AZRAEL

SPEED DATING WITH THE DENIZENS OF THE UNDERWORLD

BOOK THREE

CARRIE PULKINEN

NAUGHTY NIGHTS PRESS LLC• CANADA

AZRAEL

SPEED DATING WITH THE DENIZENS OF
THE UNDERWORLD
BOOK THREE

COPYRIGHT © 2022

CARRIE PULKINEN

ISBN: 978-1-77357-354-0

978-1-77357-355-7

PUBLISHED BY NAUGHTY NIGHTS PRESS LLC

COVER ART BY KING COVER DESIGNS

EDITED BY: KRISTA VENERO

AZRAEL

The Angel of Death needs to get a life.

Archangel Azrael—AKA the Grim Reaper—spends his life around death, and his job is taking a toll on his happiness.

At the advice of his therapist, he decides a night out with the living is just what the doctor ordered. To his dismay, it's speed dating night at DeLux Café, and the hosts refuse to let him leave.

But when a bubbly blonde vampire catches his eye, she might just be the cure to this brooding angel's woes.

Deirdre moves to LA for a change of scenery and a new flavor of the month. What better way to find Mr. Right Now than at a session of speed dating?

She sets her sights on a scrumptious dark angel, and he does not disappoint.

Deirdre has always had a hard time keeping her hands to herself, and the wicked sharp scythe glinting in the bedroom light—the object he specifically tells her not to touch—is just too tempting.

Whoops. Now she's gone from undead to really dead.

Azrael has three days to get Deirdre's soul reconnected with her body, but if she can't get over herself and forgive and forget, she'll be stuck in the spirit realm for good.

If you like sassy heroines and brooding heroes, you'll love this opposites attract paranormal romance!

Azrael is book three in the Speed Dating with the Denizens of the Underworld shared world, filled with gorgeous grim reapers, vampire vixens, and more.

CHAPTER ONE

"I GUESS BEING dead isn't all that bad." Jonathan, the spirit lying on the couch in Azrael's office, sat up and scooted to the edge of the seat. He wore the same clothes he'd died in; all souls did until they were ready to make the final transition into the spirit realm. Keeping a bit of their previous existence helped them move through the stages of grief.

"It has its benefits." Azrael rested his elbows on the arms of his cream-colored leather chair. "No physical pain."

The spirit let out a dry chuckle. "All my limbs are intact."

"Indeed they are."

"And my dick is back to normal too."

"I'm glad to hear it." The poor guy had endured a series of unfortunate events that began when he'd attempted to cast his manhood so he could make a silicone copy for his girlfriend to play with while he was away. The cast had gotten stuck, requiring surgery to remove it, and... Azrael cringed, pushing the details from his mind. There was no such thing as TMI in therapy, but damn. He could have done without knowing exactly how the penile extraction had gone. Thinking about it made his own dick want to shrivel.

"You've done well with your counseling."

Jonathan's clothing flickered. "You're a good listener."

"It's what I was made for." Yes, as the Angel of Death, Azrael did sever souls from their bodies when it was their time to go, but it wasn't as dark and menacing as people made it out to be. Well, dark maybe. Most people didn't want to die, but severing the soul was only a tiny part of Azrael's job.

His main purpose was to help the deceased transition from life to death and accept their place in the spirit realm. Azrael was a grief counselor for the dead. He also counseled supes living in Purgatory, but that was a side gig…one he'd like to do more often. Wallowing in dead people's grief could be such a downer. If humans would speak their truth while they were alive, they might not have so many regrets after death.

The spirit inhaled deeply and rose to his feet, his earthly clothes shimmering and then morphing into the standard white of a soul who'd accepted his passing.

"I'm proud of you. You'll be at peace now."

Jonathan adjusted his crotch. "So will Little John."

Azrael stood, and, trying to ignore the question of why any man would call his cock little, he placed his hand on "Big John's" shoulder, instilling his magic in the soul. Supplying an extra dose of dark angel power wasn't required for the extraction, but it made the crossing over more pleasant for the spirit.

"Thank you." Jonathan turned to mist, and the vent in the ceiling activated, sucking him out of the room and taking him to his final destination—paradise in the spirit realm.

Azrael cracked his neck and stretched his wings, the obsidian feathers reaching from wall to wall in his office. He tucked them neatly against his back before he turned toward his desk and sank into the swiveling chair behind his computer.

He clicked the appointment app and sighed as his schedule appeared on the screen. The next six souls sat firmly in the depression stage. True, he was the one who'd moved them through denial, anger, and bargaining. But it took so devil-damn long to guide spirits through the stages these days, with bargaining being the worst. Thanks to the popularity of supernatural fiction, everybody thought they could make a deal for another go on Earth. But Death didn't give second chances. Not very often, anyway.

The rewards of putting souls at rest were getting fewer and further between by the decade. Of course, it was his own fault he dealt with so many tough cases. He had plenty of dark angels, AKA reapers, working for him, but he saved the most difficult souls for himself.

He either loved a challenge or was a glutton for punishment, but it was time he made a change. He closed his laptop and strode down the hall to Jessie's office. His friend and personal counselor sat behind a clear crystal desk, typing on her computer. Her dark hair brushed her shoulders, and she wore a silk blouse with a pencil skirt in black, of course; all reapers wore black.

Azrael knocked twice on the open door before crossing the threshold. As he entered, the pale blue walls darkened to midnight, and the furniture morphed from white upholstery to black leather. His tension immediately eased with the transition, which was why the counseling center was designed this way. The magical rooms changed their façade to best suit the patients' needs.

"Hey, Boss. I'm ready for you." Jessie smiled and rose to her feet, her three-inch heels clicking on the stone floor as she strode around her desk and sank into an armchair. Fighting a smile, she glanced at the black walls and furniture. "Still into the doom and gloom, I see. We've got to work on getting some color into your life."

Azrael closed the door and sat on the chaise lounge across from her. "Black is all the colors combined. I've got plenty."

"Oh yeah. You're all rainbows and butterflies." She crossed her legs, folding her hands in her lap. "How have you been?"

He blew out a hard breath and unclenched his jaw. "The meditations ease the stress, but I..." He ground his teeth again. "I can't remember the last time I experienced happiness." And if he stayed on his current path in life, wallowing in his own misery, he'd be useless as a counselor for the dead. He'd already lost patience with the living, spending all his time either with the spirits he counseled or at home with his hellcat.

She nodded. "How long has it been since you've had sex?"

He narrowed his eyes. "A while." Truth be told, he couldn't remember the last time he'd found another being sexually appealing. Or the last time he'd had fun. "But I have no desire to find love." He'd been there, done that, gotten the t-shirt and a world of hurt to go with it.

Jessie laughed. "Who said anything about love? There's a lot to be said for one-night stands. Friends with benefits are good too, but for that, you'd actually have to have friends."

"I have friends." His brow slammed down over his eyes, his wings twitching at the accusation—more like the truth—in her words.

"Who? Samael? Ash? Have you seen them socially in the past decade?"

Azrael crossed his arms. A good therapist didn't tell you what you wanted to hear; they told you what you needed to hear...whether you liked it or not...and Jessie was the best. "So? What do you recommend?"

"You work too hard. Take some time off to enjoy life."

He scoffed. "Reapers of souls do not take vacations."

"I didn't say take a vacay, Az. Tell you what, a group of dark angels is going to DeLux tomorrow night. You should join us."

"I'd rather not." Crowds—and people in general—ruffled his feathers these days.

She sighed dramatically and rose to her feet. "Why did you come to me for counseling?"

"Because I can see where I'm headed," he grumbled. "I know I need help, and you're the best angel on my team. I trust you."

"Then *trust* me. As your therapist, I'm recommending you get out and socialize. As your friend, I'm inviting you to hang out with us at DeLux tomorrow night. Please consider it. It's time to move on." She opened the door, ending their session.

Azrael scowled, which earned him a grin and a wink. "I'll think about it."

"See you tomorrow," she called as he paced down the hall toward his office.

Jessie knew how to push every one of

his buttons, burrow under his skin, and make him see parts of himself he'd rather keep buried. It was exactly why he'd confided in the insufferable woman. She would tell it like it is, call him out when he needed it. She was the only friend he had left.

And she was right. It was time to move on. If only he could convince his heart to let go.

Azrael cared deeply for all the souls who passed through his office, and he absorbed their emotional pain, taking it inside himself to understand it, to help ease their suffering...to mask his own pain.

He was well past denial and anger, and bargaining... Ha! He'd tried to strike a deal with Lucifer himself on that one, but he'd gotten nowhere. Azrael's patients weren't the only ones planted firmly in the depression stage, but that was what he got for falling in love with a mortal. And he just had to be the one to cross her over, which meant losing her twice.

He'd known exactly what he was doing when he took on this heavy workload. Misery loved company, but it was time he put an end to his ninety-year pity party.

He *was* working too hard. So hard, in fact, that he'd abandoned his friends, conversing only with the dark angels about their jobs. Yes, Jessie was right as usual. He needed to at least *try* and socialize. He would make an appearance at DeLux tomorrow. *Damn her.*

After two more sessions with souls who weren't ready to depart, Azrael closed up shop to head home. He grabbed Severus, his scythe—which he kept secured in a closet behind his desk—and cleared his schedule, assigning the two souls booked for reaping to the new guy, Jared. Azrael was always on call for the VIP and the ornery, but Jared could take on the two scheduled to die tomorrow.

He stepped out of the counseling center and into Purgatory. Once fire and brimstone, The Underworld had gotten a makeover when Lucifer found his soulmate. Now, it looked more like a village, with houses, shops, and cafés lining the streets.

Stretching his wings to their full twelve-foot span, he gave them a flap, lifting himself from the ground. He soared over the town, enjoying the feel of the sultry Underworld wind through his feathers.

Azrael touched down in front of his home, a modest one-bedroom painted black with blacker trim. Tabitha met him at the door, winding around his legs as he entered the foyer before climbing up his pant leg.

"Hello to you too." He leaned his scythe against the wall and cradled the cat in his arms, stroking her sleek black fur. "Let me put Severus in his place, and then I'll feed you. How does salmon sound?"

Tabitha meowed her approval and leaped to the floor before darting into the bedroom. Azrael followed and set Severus in the holder by his bed, which was draped in black satin sheets—not because he was a player or a horndog...though he did know a thing or two about burying a bone—but because the color was his favorite and the material felt nice against his skin.

In the kitchen, he popped open a can of cat food and dumped it into Tabitha's bowl before giving her a scratch beneath the chin and settling onto the sofa to read. But he couldn't focus on the words. The combination of romance in the story and Jessie's advice of finding a woman made his head spin. After reading the same paragraph four times, he slammed the book shut and tossed it on the coffee table.

It had been ninety years since Nora passed. He'd done fine on his own for decades. The only woman he needed in his life was the furry little feline slinking into the room. Tabitha leaped into the armchair and licked her front paw.

Azrael patted the cushion next to him and said, "Come here, Tabs." Not that he expected a cat to come when called, but it was worth a shot. When she ignored him as usual, he rose and joined her on the chair, cradling her against his chest. "All we need is each other, right?"

Tabitha let out an irritated meow and wiggled free before darting beneath the sofa. *Typical hellcat.*

Azrael sighed, but as he felt himself slipping into a state of dejectedness, he stood. *Hell's bells, I've got to get out of the house.* The party at DeLux was more than twenty-four hours away. He needed to do something about his current mental state *now.*

After cracking the kitchen window for Tabitha, he headed out the front door and into the heart of Purgatory. A steaming cup of tarpit black coffee would hit the spot, and he could get in a little practice conversing with the living before tomorrow night. Lucifer knew he needed it.

At four in the afternoon, the only people inside the coffee shop were a demon couple and the barista. The demons sat at a small table in the corner of the room, and their chairs were so close to each other, they might as well have been in each other's laps. The two men held hands, and one of them said something that made the other's entire face light up with joy.

Azrael's chest tightened, a pang of longing making him ache. He used to smile like that a long time ago.

"What can I get for you?" The barista

tucked her bright blue hair behind her ear, revealing half a dozen piercings.

"Coffee. Tarpit black." He glanced at the couple again.

"They're sweet, aren't they?" She filled a ceramic mug. "You can tell they're soulmates. Look how they glow just being near each other."

Azrael grunted in response. Yes, he could tell.

"They just met last week too. Austin didn't have his wallet on him, so Zeke paid for his coffee. And the rest is history." She made heart eyes at the couple, and Azrael scowled.

Soulmates after only a week? Not likely for two immortals. That kind of bond took time to build. He and Nora had dated for a year before she was ready to commit to their relationship.

Sure, a year was nothing for an angel, but even then, their connection had been rocky in the beginning. It wasn't easy to make it work, but it had been well worth the effort until the end.

He paid for his coffee and sat in a chair across the room. So much for conversing with people here. He sipped the piping hot liquid from his mug, eyeing the couple over the rim. He had loved Nora with all his heart, and she loved him. Whether or not they were soulmates, he couldn't say.

Then again...

If they were, wouldn't she have chosen the immortality he'd offered and spent forever with him? Instead, she'd accepted her mortal lifespan and her eventual death. Perhaps Azrael was yet to find his soulmate. Perhaps...

He groaned, slamming the mug onto the table and causing coffee to slosh onto the surface.

"Whoopsie." The barista scurried over with a towel to soak up the mess. "Everything okay?"

"I'm fine. Sorry about the spill."

"It happens."

Azrael rose, leaving his mug half-full, and strode out the door. Anger burned in his chest, and the neutral expression he'd forced in the coffee shop pulled into another scowl. As he stomped down the main thoroughfare, more than a few people jumped out of his way.

Lucifer Fucking Morningstar. What the hell had his life become? He needed some fresh air. To get his mind right. To get his life straight.

He tucked his wings against his back,

activating his magic to hide them, and headed for the exit. When he stepped from Purgatory into the mortal world, the sun nearly blinded him, and he shielded his eyes as he took in the scene. Cars whizzed past on the busy street, and people milled about, going in and out of shops, laughing and talking.

Companionship. That was what his life was missing, what he had denied himself for decades. He'd had plenty of time to mourn his loss. Then, his isolation had become habit...one it was time he broke.

He strode through the crosswalk and wandered down the sidewalk, contemplating his existence. He hadn't known what he was missing until he fell in love with Nora. Sure, he'd been with other women before. Even angels had urges that needed to be satisfied. But now that he'd had a taste of love, he couldn't deny he missed it. Not anymore.

He meandered into Elysian Park and sat on a bench beneath a palm tree. Couples walked hand in hand down the trails, and children chased each other in a game of tag. Kids, he could do without. He had enough responsibility keeping his dark angels in line. But companionship. Someone to spend his days with...

Perhaps he was more open to that than he'd first thought.

CHAPTER TWO

WEDNESDAY EVENING FINALLY arrived, and a mix of emotions swirled in Azrael's gut as the hot water of the shower beat down on his skin. He was half dreading tonight's activities and half looking forward to a break from the mundane life he'd created for himself.

Okay, maybe three-quarters

dreading, but it was forward movement, and, like he told the souls he counseled, every baby step should be celebrated.

Water rolled down his feathers as he shut off the shower, and he gave his wings a little shake to dry them. He dressed in black jeans and...you guessed it...a black button-up. After combing his hair and putting on his shoes, he practiced his smile in the mirror.

It seemed his face had forgotten how to draw his lips upward, and it took effort to lift his permanent scowl. "Hmm. Needs work."

Tabitha meowed her agreement.

Azrael grunted. "You're no help." It was just a few drinks with friends. He could handle that. After one more attempted smile in the mirror—which looked much better than the first—he ran his hand down the cat's back and headed out the door.

The Underworld entrance to the café was a short flight over Purgatory. He gazed up at the ceiling, which didn't even begin to look like natural sky. It had been ages since he'd flown beneath the moon. Perhaps when he grew tired of the party at DeLux—which would take all of fifteen minutes at most—he'd exercise his wings over Los Angeles. If Ash or Azazel were there tonight, they might be down for a race like in the old days...before the world's first reaper of souls grew so grim.

Some time in the air topside was definitely in order. *That* he was one hundred percent looking forward to. Cool wind whipping through his feathers, the moon shining above. For the first time in as long as he could remember, a tiny tinge of excitement ignited in his chest.

He landed outside the café entrance and smoothed his hair into place before stepping inside. The interior's tile floor and globe lamps hanging from the ceiling were as he remembered, though it had been ages since he'd set foot inside. A curved staircase leading up to the mortals' floor stood along the far wall, and the drink counter ran the length of another wall. He did not, however, remember ever seeing the array of pink and red paper hearts plastered to the walls.

More hearts and cherubs in the offending colors acted as centerpieces on the tables, which were arranged in straight lines, with only two chairs at each. Heart-shaped balloons tied to every available piece of wood completed the affronting décor. It looked like Cupid himself had vomited all over the place. No, not Cupid...

"Aphrodite," Azrael grumbled as she strode toward him.

Her long brown hair flowed in loose waves over her shoulders, and she wore a tight red dress with, of course, a sweetheart neckline.

"Azrael! You're just in time." She hooked her arm around his and guided him toward a table draped in a pink cloth and covered with even more paper hearts. A giant heart with an arrow through it served as a centerpiece, and Eve shot to her feet as they approached.

"Perfect timing!" She scurried around the table, her pink dress looking identical to Aphrodite's, aside from the color. "We're short one man."

Azrael stopped in front of the table and arched a brow. "Short for what?"

"Speed dating, of course!" Eve said. "It's Wednesday."

"Oh, hell no." He'd *just* convinced himself meeting a woman might not be a bad thing. Meeting twenty in one night, however, would be torture. Finding a soulmate should happen naturally, by accident, like the demon couple from the coffee shop. Not from perusing a buffet of candidates.

Azrael tried for an escape, but Aphrodite hung tight to his arm, while Eve clutched the other. He cast his gaze to the bar, where Jessie sat with another dark angel. She smiled and mouthed the words, "Have fun," lifting her drink in a toast.

He'd been tricked.

"This is not happening." He tugged from the women's grip. "Find someone else."

"Please, hon?" Eve patted his arm before picking up a card filled with names. "We need an even number for it to work."

He glared at Jessie, and, out of the corner of his eye, he caught a glimpse of Lucifer. *Fuck me.* The man-in-charge inclined his chin, giving Azrael a look that said if he didn't comply, there would be literal hell to pay.

Azrael inhaled deeply, closing his eyes before letting out a long, slow breath. He would be having words with Jessie tomorrow. "How does it work?"

"Start at table five." Eve handed him

the card. "Then move clockwise at the buzzer to meet each woman. You get five minutes to get to know them, and you can take notes on your card to remind you whom you made a connection with."

He would not be making a connection with anyone—who could in only five minutes' time?—but he knew better than to cross Lucifer. "Where's table five?"

"Right over there." Aphrodite pointed. "But wait with the other men for a minute first, and most of all...have fun!"

Yeah, right.

***

Deirdre Boudreaux parked her custom pink Ford Mustang in a lot two blocks from DeLux Café and pulled down the visor to check her makeup. The light next to the small mirror flicked on, and she smiled. Her shimmery pink eyeshadow accented her sky-blue eyes perfectly, and her brows were on point.

Her gaze dropped to her mouth to inspect the new Magenta Millions lipstick she'd bought online at Neiman Marcus, and her smile slipped into a frown. The bright pink lip color coated the tips of her fangs, making it look like she'd fed on a unicorn and forgotten to brush her teeth.

"I knew I should've stuck with the lip stain. Fangs and normal lipstick do not play nicely together." She pulled a tissue from her purse and cleaned her lips and tips before applying her old standby: Perilously Pink 18-Hour Lip Stain.

With any luck, she'd have to reapply before she sent her next ex-lover on his way.

AZRAEL

She adjusted her boobs in her corset, making sure the zipper was engaged. There wouldn't be any nip slips until she was ready for them. "Let the games begin."

Deirdre's strappy Louboutin stilettos cradled her feet as she strode across the intersection, and a man in a Lamborghini lowered his tinted window to whistle. She ignored him, setting her sights on the bouncer standing outside the café. He was tall and beefy, and his veins protruded on his neck and arms like he hit the gym a few too many times a week.

Her mouth watered as she approached, and she ran her tongue over the tip of one fang. Good thing she fed before she arrived. She was here for a date, not a snack.

The bouncer gave her a once-over and held out his hand. "ID please?"

She flashed her fangs. "I'm here for the speed dating."

"ID."

Normally in a club for supes, her fangs were all the ID she needed. She was more than two hundred years old, after all. Rather than argue, she tugged the fake document from her purse and handed it to him.

He arched a brow. "Twenty-seven?"

She shrugged. "Give or take a few hundred."

He handed it back to her. "Purgatory level is down the stairs and through the red curtain. Have fun."

"Oh, I plan to." She entered the building and paused. The upstairs portion swarmed with humans getting ready for their round of speed dating. Pink and red hearts and balloons decorated the mostly white café, the splash of Deirdre's favorite color a perfect complement to the event.

Her heels clicked on the tile as she sashayed down the staircase, and she pulled the red velvet curtain aside to enter the Underworld portion of the club. To her delight, the same Valentine-themed decorations were spread throughout the space, making her feel right at home.

A table draped in pink sat off to the left, and a vampire with long, wavy hair nearly the same shade of blonde as Deirdre's sat behind it. "Welcome. It's nice to see another vampire in the club. I'm Eve."

"Deirdre. Nice to meet you." She took

in Eve's outfit, a pink dress with a sweetheart neckline. She may have found her first vamp friend in L.A. A pink metal heart with an arrow through it acted as a centerpiece on the table, and Deirdre picked it up to examine it.

"Don't touch that." Eve took it from her hands and returned it to the table. "Aphrodite can be...particular about her decorations."

"Sorry." Deirdre brushed her hair behind her shoulder. "Bad habit."

"I love your corset," Eve said.

"Thanks. Pink is my favorite color."

"I don't know why everyone assumes vampires only like black and red. Nothing could be further from the truth." Eve picked up a pale pink card and a pen. "You look like a woman who's ready to speed date."

Deirdre rested a hand on her hip, shifting her weight to one foot. "Fast and fabulous. How do I sign up?"

Eve wrote a number on the card and handed it to her. "We'll put you at table two. The women stay put, and the men will rotate at the buzzer. You can take notes on each date to help you remember who you'd like to spend more time with."

"Sounds like fun." Deirdre stopped by the bar to order a glass of blood. The menu revealed every variety under the moon. *Fancy.* She'd never had the opportunity to order such a rare type as AB negative before.

The price was outrageous, which seemed the norm for this city, but she bought it anyway. *When in Rome...* She took her seat and grinned at the woman next to her.

"First time?" The woman returned the smile.

"Is it that obvious?"

She laughed. "It goes fast, so be sure to take notes. They all seem to bleed into one after a while. Oh." She pressed her fingers to her lips. "No pun intended."

"Sounds like fun to me." Deirdre scanned the crowd, observing her upcoming dates as they conversed by the bar. Several potential prospects caught her eye, but none lit a fire in her...yet. That could change when she got to know them, even if she only had five minutes to do so.

Contrary to popular belief, she did require a nice personality in her boyfriends. So what if she never kept them around longer than a month?

Those thirty days needed to be filled with fun, laughter...and sex, of course. Lots and lots of sex.

She always ended her relationships before the men could get too attached. Before *she* could get attached. Getting turned into a vampire by the man she loved and then being abandoned after only five years did a number on a woman. Go figure.

Still, lust at first sight could be so exciting. It had been a while since she'd experienced the sensation.

She crossed her legs, wiggling her foot in anticipation. "Let's get this show on the road," she said under her breath. "Some of us have to be home before sunrise. *Long* before, if things go well tonight."

Her spine straightened as her gaze

landed on a scrumptious man near the entrance. Tall, dark, and delectable, he wore all black and had a set of onyx wings tucked against his back. He had short brown hair, dark broody eyes, and a broad chest that hinted at a muscular frame. He hadn't entered through the velvet curtain, which meant he'd come straight from the Underworld. She had found herself an Angel of Death. *Yummy.*

A woman in red with long brown hair clung to his arm, and Deirdre hoped to Hades she wasn't his date. Because A: Who brought a date to speed dating? And B: Deirdre had found her lust at first sight.

He seemed reluctant to take the card Eve offered him, and as he turned to walk away, she rose and clutched his arm. He shook his head as if he didn't want to join the fun, and if Deirdre's glamour would have worked at such a long distance, she'd have tickled his mind just enough to make him want to come.

Because Lilith help her, she wanted to make this man *come*.

She pursed her lips. Honestly, she wasn't sure if glamour would work on a dark angel, but she would love to try. Then again, with the strength of her feminine wiles, she'd never needed to glamour a man to get him into her bed, nor would she ever resort to such archaic tactics.

The sexy-hot angel finally accepted the card, and Eve's smile beamed as she took a microphone, then steered him toward the group of men. "Okay, guys and gals," she announced, "you all know the rules, so, gentlemen, take your places and let the fun begin!"

The angel took a seat three tables away from her, and she held in her sigh of frustration. It would be a while before he made it all the way back around to table two, so she focused her gaze on the beefy, hairy man who sat down in front of her.

"Hi. I'm Dale." His voice was deep and rumbly like a wolf's growl.

"Well, hello, handsome." She leaned an elbow on the table, and his gaze dropped to the cleavage emerging from her corset, as expected. With two hundred years of dating experience, she knew how to dress for the occasion...and how to get what she wanted. "I'm Deirdre, and you must be a werewolf."

"Guilty," he chuckled. "What gave it

away? It was the chest hair, wasn't it?"

Deirdre glanced at the angel, who looked like he was fighting a scowl as the woman at his table chatted away. Poor guy. The vampire of his wet and wildest dreams was right here waiting for him, yet he had to endure the full circle of dates before he'd find her. Deirdre's lips curled, and she shifted her focus back to her current date. "That, and your scent. Shifters tend to smell like their animals, even in human form."

He crossed his arms, looking offended. "Will that be a problem?"

She lifted one shoulder dismissively. "That depends on what you're looking for."

"I'm in the market for a mate." He angled his chin upward as if challenging her to accept.

"Then I'm afraid you're barking up the wrong tree, wolfman. I'm only here for a fling." And she intended for her next flavor of the month to be dark and delicious.

"Hmph." Dale had circled her name on his card when he sat down, but now he drew an X through it. "Sorry to waste your time."

The men made their rounds, and while Deirdre tried to give each potential date her full attention, she couldn't help but steal glances at her angel. And he would be *her* angel by the end of the night. He was two seats away when a tall, pale vampire glided into the chair across from her.

"Hello, *ma chère*. My name is Gaston. It's a pleasure to make your acquaintance." He wore his long dark hair tied back in a band, and his sapphire shirt matched his icy blue eyes.

Deirdre arched an eyebrow. If her angel didn't work out, this man could be her Plan B.

"I must front up to you and say that I'm only in L.A. for the week." He took a sip from his goblet and set it on the table.

She tilted her head. "Do you mean 'be up front'?"

He smiled, showing fang. "That is what I said."

"Well, that's good to hear because I'm only looking for a fling."

"Good indeed." He took another drink from his glass.

"Have you tried the AB negative?" She circled her finger over the rim of hers. "It's divine."

"Especially mixed with a heavy dose of their craft whiskey. They don't serve them like this back home."

She'd considered adding a shot to hers, but she decided she'd better not. It was best to keep her wits about her when interviewing potential one-night— or month-long—stands. "Where are you from?"

"The greatest city in the world, of course. New Orleans. I've lived there as long as the city has been in existence."

Deirdre let out a slow breath. She had recently moved from New Orleans to get away from everything she'd lost. No way in all of Purgatory was she going to rekindle that pain by sleeping with someone from her hometown.

"I'm sorry, Gaston, but I am afraid southern boys just aren't my cup of blood."

"Perhaps you've simply been drinking from the wrong vessels."

She laughed. "I've tried every cup, chalice, glass, and mason jar out there. Believe me when I say *this*..." She gestured from him to herself. "Isn't going to happen."

Before he could say more, the buzzer sounded, and he rose, bowing slightly and moving on to the woman next to her.

Her next seemingly endless date babbled on and on about himself, sweat beading on his forehead and soaking his pits. She hardly heard a word he said. Then it happened.

The buzzer sounded, and her angel took the seat across from her. "Hello." He glanced at the timer on the wall and said nothing more.

"Well, aren't you silent and scrumptious? I'm Deirdre. What's your name?"

"Azrael."

She laughed, unable to help herself. "Really? Have you caught any Smurfs lately?"

He furrowed his brow. "What do you mean?"

"You know. The little blue guys who live in a mushroom village." He looked confused, so she continued, "Gargamel?"

He shook his head. "Never heard of him."

"Boy, you don't get out of the Underworld much, do you?"

He squared his gaze on her, his dark brown eyes seeming to penetrate to her soul and making her shiver. "Not nearly enough, it seems."

She swallowed the lump forming in her throat. "I'm sorry. I shouldn't have made fun of your name. It's not your fault your parents named you after a cartoon cat." She poked her tongue with a fang. *That wasn't any better, Dee. Give the man a break.*

He let out a dry chuckle. "I assure you I am not named after a cartoon."

"It's okay if you are. I'm named after some tragic heroine from an Irish legend."

He glowered. "I am not named after anyone. I'm the Angel of Death. The *Archangel of Death.*"

"Wow. Like *the* man in charge? The Grim Reaper?" *Sweet Lilith.* Dark, broody, *and* powerful? That didn't just tip the sexy meter in his favor; the mercury burst out the top and was pooling at his feet. If she wasn't careful, she'd be joining the liquid metal as a blob of melted goo on the floor.

"That would be me, though the reaper name can be used for all my dark angels." His gaze drifted to her cleavage briefly before returning to her eyes, and something sparked in his.

Gotcha. Even though she'd offended him, he'd taken the bait. Now she just had to hook him with her wiles. Yes, she used her boobs as man-bait. If she were looking for something serious—which she wasn't, nor would she ever be—she'd rethink her game. But the quickest way into a man's pants was through his eyes, so she used her assets to her advantage.

She leaned forward, resting her arms on the table. "What brings *the* Angel of

Death to speed dating? I'd think with your power and good looks, you could get any woman you wanted."

"I didn't come for speed dating. I got roped into it when I arrived here." He glanced at the timer again, and when he looked into her eyes, his demeanor shifted ever so slightly, the tension in his shoulders easing. "I spend too much time with the dead, and my therapist suggested I get out and experience the living for a change."

His therapist? She'd never dated a man who was actually in touch with his feelings. *How intriguing.* "I'm not exactly living. Do I count?"

He leaned back, sweeping his smoldering gaze down her form. "You look *very* alive to me, Deirdre."

Hot damn. She brushed her hand

across her stomach to make sure all her clothes hadn't fallen off on their own.

His eyes widened, and he shook his head as if he hadn't meant to say that out loud. "You don't sound like you grew up in L.A. Where are you from?"

"Where do I sound like I'm from?" she drawled.

"The South."

She laughed. "Louisiana is a southern state, but New Orleans has an accent all its own. Have you ever been?"

"I've been everywhere. What brought you here?"

She lifted one shoulder seductively. "Speed dating sounded like fun."

"What brought you to L.A.? I assume you used the topside entrance to get down here."

"Ah. I suppose I needed a change of

scenery. I'd spent my entire existence in New Orleans, after all. When you can live forever, you need to get out and experience the world."

He tilted his head. "Is that the only reason?"

"Well, I—" For some devil-damned reason, she nearly opened up and told him way more about herself than anyone needed to know. Thankfully, the buzzer sounded, saving her from making that grave mistake. "Can I give you my number, *cher*? I'd love to...talk...some more."

He rose and rested his hands on the back of the chair, hesitating slightly before he spoke. "Like I said, I got roped into this because they were short one man. It was nice to meet you, Deirdre."

Before she could respond, he moved

on to the next table. She sat there with her mouth hanging open until her new date sat down in front of her. A tiny sliver of pain cracked open in her chest, reminding her of the only other time she'd been rejected. *Oh, hell no.*

She refused to let that wound fester again. Mr. Sexy Hot Angel wanted her; she could tell by the look in his eyes and the way his pheromones flared. She could smell his desire, and it was the warmest, most masculine scent she'd ever encountered. There simply hadn't been enough time for him to get to know her, and there was only one way to remedy that.

CHAPTER THREE

AZRAEL ENDURED HIS last two dates and made a beeline for the stairs. Activating his magic, he hid his wings as he paced through the human level of DeLux Café, heading straight for the topside exit.

That woman...

With her blonde hair and bright blue

eyes, her pink corset and creamy skin that begged to be touched... Her smile made her entire face sparkle to the point he figured glitter probably shot out her ass every time she farted.

She was the epitome of life, yet she was undead. How ironic.

This entire night had been a setup. As far as Jessie knew, he didn't want to date, yet she'd convinced him to come on speed dating night, neglecting to give him that important piece of information. Hell, she'd even conspired with Aphrodite, Eve, and Lucifer himself to make it happen, and not a single woman had piqued his interest, as expected, until Deirdre.

Her charm had disarmed him. He'd let his guard down, and he had nearly flirted with her. Nearly let her know she intrigued him. Looking at her had made something come to life in his core, and he wasn't sure what to do about it.

It had been so long...

He should have accepted her number when she offered it. At least then he'd have the option to see her again if and when he decided to pursue the one-night stand Jessie had prescribed.

It was just as well he didn't. Right now, he needed to clear his head, and the best way to do that was by taking to the sky. He shoved open the door and stepped onto the sidewalk, gazing up at the full moon hanging high above the city. A car horn blared in the distance, and a cool autumn breeze tickled his invisible feathers.

His wings twitched with the urge to fly, and while he'd hidden them from the mortals' view, he couldn't very well take flight right in front of all these humans. He strode toward the crosswalk, heading for the park, and then he spotted her.

She stood at least six feet tall with her heels on, and his stomach clenched as thoughts of where her lips would align with his flashed behind his eyes. Her smile made his heart race. She strode toward him with the assertive gait of a woman who knew exactly what she wanted. Yet for all her confidence and cheer, he detected a hint of unresolved sadness buried deep beneath the surface.

He steeled himself as she approached. She wasn't a soul who needed counseling, and he wasn't ready for a woman who radiated so much light.

"There you are. I was looking for you."

She rested a hand on her hip, drawing his attention to her curvy figure. "I'm glad we bumped into each other again."

"Why were you looking for me topside?"

"You said you wanted to spend time with the living." She lifted one shoulder as if the answer were obvious. "Since the speed dating was torturous for you, I figured you'd want some fresh air."

"Hmm." He narrowed his eyes. She was beautiful *and* she listened. A wriggling formed in the back of his mind, warning him he was about to get in over his head. He felt too much for this woman, which was completely ridiculous. He'd known her for five minutes.

"I'm not wrong," she sang, flashing her heart-melting smile.

The energy she exuded was contagious, and the corners of his mouth lifted slightly in response. "No, you're not. But I meant it when I said I didn't come here for dating."

"Who said anything about dating? I'm certainly not looking for a relationship." Her fangs brushed her bottom lip, and he couldn't help but imagine what they might feel like grazing his skin, nipping at his tender spots...

The wriggling in his mind intensified, and he wondered if Fate didn't have a hand in this meeting. Was this what it felt like to find a soulmate? The demon couple from the coffee shop clicked quickly, so it might be possible...

He let his gaze wander over her form. What was he thinking? Fate wouldn't send him a woman who was his polar opposite. This was the first time he'd put himself out there in decades. The emotions stirring in his soul were simply the product of a too-long celibate man finding a woman attractive. Nothing more.

"How about this?" she asked when he didn't reply. "I'm new in town and haven't seen much of the city. Why don't you show me some of your favorite places, and we'll see where it goes from there?"

He shouldn't. He'd come topside to stretch his wings and fly beneath the moon, not play tour guide to a woman so bright she could burn him to ash. He knew exactly where she wanted it to go from there. If he were honest with himself, he'd admit he might want it to lead to the same place.

Hell's bells. I'm going to regret this.
"How about I show you the entire city?"
He motioned toward the crosswalk as
the indicator flipped from a red hand to
a green stick figure.

She grinned and followed his lead. "I
like your ambition, but I have to be
home before dawn. I'm allergic to the
sun."

"Allergic?" He glanced at her as they
crossed the intersection.

"It'll burn me alive."

He paused on the sidewalk and faced
her. "I promise to have you home well
before sunrise."

An errant strand of blonde hair fell
across her forehead, and without
thinking, he brushed it aside. Their
gazes met, and the action felt far more
intimate than he'd intended. He jerked

his hand to his side. "We'll start in Elysian Park. This way."

What are you doing, Az? He'd cursed Jessie all evening for trying to set him up, and now he'd willingly fallen into her trap. Still, he couldn't shake the unnerving feeling that Fate was also involved. *That's hellhound shit. It doesn't happen this way. Not this fast.* But, like Deirdre suggested, it wouldn't hurt to see where things went. Hell, he deserved to have some fun, and she seemed free-spirited enough to enjoy what he had to offer.

She matched his strides, keeping pace with him as he turned down a side street and headed away from the crowds outside the clubs. "We're walking kinda fast for sightseeing, aren't we?"

"We won't be walking for long." He

slowed his pace and glanced at her high heels as they reached the park entrance. "Do you need to take a break?"

She laughed. "I'm a vampire, and we're walking at a mortal's pace. I'm fine."

"Even in those shoes?"

"Especially in these shoes."

"In that case..." He broke into a run.

Why he did it, he wasn't sure, but as she caught up to him and asked, "Is this all you've got?" a flush of adrenaline hummed in his veins. He poured on the speed, racing her down a paved path lined with palm trees, deeper into the park.

He stopped as they reached the beginning of the hiking trail and arched a brow at her. "Now do you need a break?"

"I'm not even winded." She winked and crossed her arms. "What else have you got?"

"Are you up for a short hike?"

"Hmm... A hike in the woods, in the dark, with the Angel of Death. That sounds perfectly safe."

"I left my scythe at home. I'm harmless." He winked, and his lips curved upward even more.

"No wooden stakes in your back pockets?"

"Cross my heart." He drew an X over his chest.

Deirdre pursed her lips, eyeing him as if deciding whether she could take him if he tried something. He had no doubt she'd be a formidable opponent in a fight. All vampires had otherworldly strength and stamina. But the only staking he had in mind would involve him burying his wood balls-deep inside her. A shiver shimmied up his spine at the thought. Whether it was Fate or simply his libido finally coming out of hibernation, he *wanted* this woman.

"Why not?" She shrugged. "I've already died once. I doubt it will happen again. My second life would be absolutely boring without a little danger."

"Shall we?" He offered his hand, and she took it. Her skin was cool to the touch, not as frigid as a ghost, but she lacked the warmth of the living. He found it oddly attractive. Truth be told, he found everything about her appealing, especially her sense of adventure.

"Look at me, flirting with Death." She

walked by his side up the trail, the dry, packed earth having no effect on her high heels. In fact, she moved so smoothly, he wondered if her feet even touched the ground. She had the grace of a feline with a contagious energy that excited him in more ways than one.

As they reached the top of the hill, her breath caught. A single swing hung from a towering tree, overlooking an expanse of the city below. Lights from the houses twinkled like stars in the darkness, disappearing into the horizon and making it hard to tell where Earth ended and the heavens began.

She released his hand to clutch the ropes holding the swing. "What a view."

He stood behind her. "I hope you're not afraid of heights."

"We're not *that* high."

"Not yet." He unfurled his wings, stretching them outward to their full twelve-foot span.

She spun around, and her eyes widened as she took them in. "You're not suggesting we go flying, are you?"

He hesitated, his stomach tightening. *You knew what you were doing when you brought her up here, Az. You can't back out now.* He opened his arms. "I am. Have you ever flown before?"

"Never." Her gaze traveled down his body before returning to his eyes. "I don't suppose you have a magical harness in your pocket? How will I keep from falling?"

"I'll hold you. I promise not to let you fall."

She stepped toward him and placed her hands on his biceps, giving them a squeeze. "You definitely feel strong enough."

"Do you trust me?"

"Absolutely not. I've known you all of a half-hour, but I'd be a fool to pass up the chance to fly with an angel. Just don't drop me on anything sharp."

"Brave woman."

"Or incredibly stupid. I'll let you know which when we're done."

"Turn around." As she faced the city below, he held her, one arm around her hips, the other around her chest, just below her breasts. With her back pressed to his front, he tightened his hold, and the scent of her floral shampoo filled his senses.

It had been years since he'd held a woman. Hell, it had been decades since he'd found someone this appealing. He willed his dick into submission, and his lips brushed her ear as he asked, "Are you ready?"

Goosebumps rose on her skin. "Hell yeah, I am."

He flapped his wings, and she squealed as they rose from the ground. "Don't worry," he said. "I've got you."

They took to the sky and soared over the city, the feel of the cool autumn wind on his wings and the view of the moon above exhilarating him. This was exactly what he needed to get out of the rut his life had become. He didn't need speed dating. Hell, he didn't need to go to DeLux Café at all. All he'd needed was the open sky.

Although...he had to admit, the woman in his arms did add to thrill. Okay, she was a huge part of it. *Fuck.*

She *was* the thrill.

"This is amazing!" Deirdre stretched her arms out to her sides, and as he flapped his wings, his feathers brushed her fingertips. She gasped. "They're so soft."

She turned her hands palms up, and he flapped again, moving his wings forward and back so she could feel their texture. Her touch sent vibrating energy rushing from his feathers to his back before it spread into his chest.

His entire body hummed. An angel's wings were a sacred part of him. Allowing someone to touch them, to caress the feathers like Deirdre did, was an act as intimate as sex...and he wanted more.

"You weren't kidding when you said you'd show me the whole city. A girl could get addicted to this kind of rush."

"You haven't seen anything yet." He angled upward, taking her higher before tucking his wings against his back and free falling.

"Holy shit!" She clutched his arm with both hands.

"Do you want me to stop us?"

"Not until you absolutely have to. Woo!"

He let the free fall last a few more moments before opening his wings and catching the wind. Her grip loosened, but she didn't move her hands from his arm as they floated toward the ground. As his feet touched soil, he held on to her, both because her legs were probably trembling from the flight and because he enjoyed the way she felt pressed against him.

"Can you stand?" he asked.

"I think so." She held on to his arm as she stepped out of his embrace and turned to face him. "Thank you for that. When you're immortal, adrenaline rushes are hard to come by."

"I know exactly what you mean." He trailed his fingers down her cheek.

She caught his hand before he could drop it and held it in both of hers. "That excited me in more ways than one, if you catch my drift."

Oh, he caught it...and he wanted to ride it all night long. Without thinking, without considering the consequences, he leaned in and kissed her.

CHAPTER FOUR

HOLY HELLHOUNDS, DEATH tasted as sinful as he looked. This brooding dark angel was turning out to be a rollercoaster of excitement. Deirdre linked her hands behind his neck, pulling him closer, and man oh man, did his body feel good pressed to hers. He was hard *all over*, especially the rod in his jeans, which she had every intention of impaling herself with once she got him home.

His lips were soft as silk, and as they parted, her tongue brushing his, she caught the faintest hint of cinnamon, warm and inviting. He wrapped his arms around her and glided one hand up to cradle the back of her head. For a hot minute, she thought he was going to be a gentle lover with how soft his touch was. Then he slid his other hand down to her ass and squeezed, a deep, masculine groan vibrating in his chest as he tangled his fingers in her hair.

Game on.

She pulled away, smiling playfully, and ran a finger down his chest. "You promised to take me home well before daylight."

Azrael arched a brow, his gaze wandering down her body before returning to her eyes. "What about your car?"

"It'll be fine in the lot. I can get it tomorrow."

He narrowed his eyes, considering her.

No way in hell was she letting this fine specimen of a man get away without having *her way* with him first. He was too scrumptious to pass up. "You could fly us to my apartment. There's a secluded alleyway we could land in, and no one will be the wiser." She bit her bottom lip and flashed him her most seductive look.

His full lips curled into a crooked smile. "A woman after my own heart."

"I'm not interested in your heart,

cher. The rest of your body, though..."
She brushed her fingertips along his wing, and he closed his eyes, inhaling deeply as if her touch was the most exquisite thing he'd ever felt.

As his eyes opened, he clutched her shoulder, turning her around before picking her up and taking to the sky. She gasped as they ascended, the wind in her hair and the feel of his arms wrapped around her exhilarating to no end.

A human would have been terrified soaring to such heights, but not Deirdre. One: this dark angel had the strength of an immortal, and for some unknown reason, she trusted him not to drop her. Two: even if he did drop her, as long as she didn't end up impaled on a fence post or without her head, she'd survive the fall. Sure, it would hurt like hell, but the hint of danger added to the rush.

"Where do you live?" His lips brushed her ear as he spoke, and she shivered.

"555 Maple. Ground floor."

He angled his wings, taking them across town before dropping quickly into the alley between buildings. Her knees wobbled, and she clung to his arm to steady herself.

He didn't seem to mind, as he nuzzled into her hair, inhaling deeply and sliding his other hand down her hip. "This is the part where you invite me inside."

She grinned and stepped from his embrace, turning around and brushing her hair behind her shoulder. "What if I've changed my mind?"

He chuckled. "You haven't."

"But if I had?"

He cupped her cheek in his hand, brushing her skin with his thumb. "Then I would bid you goodnight and fly away. Is that what you want?"

"Hell no. Let's go." She clutched his hand and led him through the building entrance toward her door. With a sly grin, she unlocked it and let it swing open. "Now this is the part where you rock my world."

"Get ready for one hell of a brush with Death."

As they crossed the threshold, he kicked the door shut and shoved her against it before crushing his mouth to hers. If she were human, the act might've been too rough. But, being a vampire, she could withstand just about anything he could dish out, and, Lilith have mercy, his forcefulness heated her body to the core.

She fumbled for the lock and twisted it before taking his face in her hands and kissing him like he was the last drop of blood on Earth. Speaking of blood...she'd never tasted an angel before.

Breaking the kiss, she glided her lips along his jaw before swiping her tongue down the side of his neck. She could practically smell the warm, coppery liquid through his skin, could almost taste it...

Nope. She couldn't. Well, technically, she could if she wanted to—and boy oh boy did she ever want to—but she shouldn't. She'd ruined one too many nights of fun by biting too soon when she was younger, and she had learned her lesson.

Sexy times first. Snack time later.

Okay, and maybe since he was *the* Angel of Death, she'd get his permission before she partook in the delicious life force pulsing through his veins. *Whatever. A girl's gotta eat.*

Azrael found her mouth with his once more, and he squeezed her ass with one hand while cupping a breast in the other. The warmth of his palms penetrated the fabric of her clothes. There was too much fabric between them...and not enough penetration.

She yanked his shirt out of his pants and undid the buttons before pressing her hands to his chest. Soft skin, hard muscles. *Yum.* Running her fingers over his shoulders, she tugged his shirt downward, but it got hung up on his wings.

"How on earth do you get dressed with those things?"

He chuckled and grabbed the collar behind his neck, pulling it up over his head, and she glimpsed a breakaway panel with a cutout for his wings.

"Clever," she mused, "but with a body like that, I don't know why you bother with clothes."

"I'm sure it would make my clients uncomfortable to be counseled by a half-naked angel."

"Counseled? I thought you reaped souls and delivered them to the Underworld."

"I'm also a grief counselor for the dead." He reached for the zipper on her corset and yanked it down in one swift pull.

She let it fall to the floor, a little shiver running up her spine as his pupils dilated and his tongue slipped out to moisten his lips. Sweet Lilith, he'd practically devoured her with his eyes alone.

"Why would the dead be grieving?" She unzipped her pants and shimmied out of them, kicking them next to her corset.

"Because they're dead." He cupped her breasts, teasing her nipples with his thumbs until they hardened beneath his touch.

The sensation tingled through her body, and she tipped her head back, closing her eyes as he dipped his head and took a nipple into his mouth. "Mmm..." She unbuttoned his jeans and worked them over his hips and down his thighs before palming his dick through his black briefs.

He sucked in a sharp breath and toed off his shoes, kicking his pants aside. Now it was Deirdre's turn to lick her lips. The man had a body that was sculpted like a...well, like an angel. Gliding her hand up then down, she slipped her fingers into his underwear, wrapping them around his cock. *Damn, talk about a bone.* She couldn't wait to help him bury it.

Azrael let out a masculine groan and lifted her from the floor before carrying her deeper into the apartment. She clung to his neck, kissing him with everything she had as she wrapped her legs around his waist. He stopped in the kitchen and planted her on the countertop. His hands felt hot against her death-chilled skin, the moist heat of his tongue blazing a trail of fire across her chest. She ran her hands along the tops of his wings, and he shuddered, pulling away and looking at her with passion-drunk eyes.

"Tell me what you want." The deep rumble of his voice vibrated through her soul.

"I want you to ram your stake so hard inside me, I forget my own name."

He grunted and slid her off the counter before turning her around and yanking her panties down to her ankles. Kicking them aside, she spread her legs and bent over, peering at him over her shoulder. He ran a hand down her back, trailing his fingers around her hip to brush her clit.

Electricity ricocheted through her

core as he circled her nub, and when he slipped two fingers inside her, she gripped the edges of the counter and leaned into him, taking them deeper. He stroked her sweet spot a few more times before pressing his tip against her and sliding in with one swift thrust.

She moaned as he filled her, his thick shaft stretching her to a pleasurable ache. Gripping her hips, he slid out slowly and slammed into her again. The feel of his skin slapping against hers nearly made her come.

"You are so fucking beautiful, Deirdre." He pumped his hips, the delectable friction making her scream his name.

"Oh, Azrael!"

His wings unfurled, stretching nearly from wall to wall and sending a crystal vase on the far counter tumbling to the floor. It shattered on impact, and he froze. "I'm sorry. Sometimes my wings have a mind of their own."

"No worries." She straightened, his cock slipping out of her as she turned. "Let's take this to the bedroom. I feel like going for a ride." She gave his dick two firm strokes before making a come-here motion with her fingers and leading him to her bed.

He took her in his arms and kissed her again, his warm cinnamon scent filling her senses and creating a sort of calm she couldn't recall ever feeling before. She leaned into him, backing him up until his legs met the mattress. They fell to the bed together, his wings outstretched beneath them, giving him an ethereal beauty that took her breath away.

She straddled his groin, and, rising onto her knees, she guided him to her folds and sheathed him. His eyes smoldered as she rode him, his gaze never straying from hers. With a wicked grin, he licked his thumb and pressed it to her clit, stroking it in gentle circles along with her movements.

Her orgasm coiled inside her, tightening her muscles in exquisite agony before releasing in an explosion of ecstasy. She cried out his name again, and he gripped her hips, thrusting harder and faster until he joined her in heaven.

Panting—and it took a lot to make a vampire pant—she rose and then lay by his side, resting her head on his shoulder. His feathers felt like down beneath her.

"Is it okay if I lie here on your wing?"

He inhaled deeply and turned his head toward her. Pressing a kiss to her forehead, he lifted his wing, moving her closer to his body and angling it forward to wrap around her. The strange sense of calm washed over her again, and she draped her leg across his hips.

"I'll take that as a yes." She gently clutched one of his feathers, running her hand down to the tip.

"Yes." He let out an unbelieving chuckle. "Oddly...yes."

"Why is it odd?" She traced her fingers along his stomach, and his muscles tightened with her touch.

"An angel's wings are one of the most intimate parts of his body. They're full of nerve endings, and we don't let just anyone touch them." He lifted his wing and brushed his feathers up her leg. "But you aren't just anyone."

Her stomach fluttered at the idea that he found her worthy, which was utterly ridiculous. He hardly knew her. "I bet you say that to all your one-night-stands."

"I assure you I do not. Nor do I have many one-night stands."

She lifted her head to look at him. "How would you keep someone you're sleeping with from touching them?"

"I would tuck them into my back and use my magic to make them disappear."

"But you didn't do that with me."

"I didn't feel the need."

"Why?"

"I wish I knew the answer to that."

"Hmm." She rested her head on his

shoulder. This dark angel was sexy enough to keep around for a while, but she didn't dare. Anytime she felt this strongly about a man in such a short time, it meant he needed to be a one-and-done deal. She'd given her heart away once. It was a mistake she would never make again. She rose from the bed and slipped on a pink silk robe.

Azrael sat up and folded his wings behind him. "I am sorry about your vase. I'll replace it for you."

She sank onto the edge of the bed and kissed his cheek. "No need. It's not real crystal anyway. I bought it at Target."

She rested her palm against his face. "It'll be daylight soon, and then I'll be dead to the world for eight hours. If you want me to walk you to the door, you better get dressed."

He took her hand and brought it to his lips. "What if I want to stay?"

She smiled and shook her head. "You don't."

CHAPTER FIVE

AZRAEL SAT BEHIND his desk in the counseling center, finishing the weekly schedule and assigning the next round of souls for his angels to reap. With no clients present, the décor matched his own style, with black marble floors, charcoal walls, and onyx leather furniture.

He'd woken early, despite staying out late with Deirdre, and he'd arrived at the office long before any of his angels showed up.

Deirdre...

Simply being near the seductive vampire had unleashed a side of him he'd forgotten existed. And the way it felt when she touched him...

His phone pinged with a notification, drawing him from his thoughts before he could get himself worked up again, and that was a good thing. He'd already played their evening over in his mind this morning and had to take care of himself in the shower.

He peered at his phone, and the name of his next client popped onto the screen. Joey Sinclair's time on Earth had expired, but the stubborn bastard refused to let go. A billionaire hedge fund manager in charge of even more people's billions, to say he was a control freak was an understatement. Azrael expected Joey to remain in denial for at least a decade, which was why he'd taken him on as a client rather than assigning him to one of his reaper counselors.

He rose and grabbed Severus from its spot in the closet. The scythe's magic hummed in his hands, and he drew it inward, using its power to whisk him into the angelic plane, where he could simply picture where he wanted to go, and he'd arrive on Earth in an instant.

In a cloak of magic, he landed next to Joey's bed in his mansion. The man lay alone in the room, hooked up to several hospital-grade machines, which were keeping him alive. A feeding tube went in through his nose, and two bags of fluids dripped into his bloodstream through IVs. His spirit clung loosely to his body, pulsating softly with Azrael's presence.

"What are you doing here? It's not my time," his spirit spoke, while his body remained still.

"I'm afraid it *is* your time, my friend. I'll be taking you to Purgatory now and preparing you for the transition to the spirit world."

Panic laced his voice. "But I still have things to do. I have money to manage. I haven't..."

Azrael swiped his scythe against Joey's body. The magical instrument never harmed the flesh; it severed the soul from the physical form, freeing it from its restraints.

Joey gasped, his spirit standing next

to Azrael as the heart rate monitor let out a long, steady *beeeeep*. "No," he whispered. "This can't be happening."

Azrael rested a hand on his shoulder. "Everyone dies." Well, that was true for mortals, anyway. "Denial is a normal stage after death. I'm here to help you through it."

Joey scoffed and raked his gaze down Azrael's form. "Oh? The Grim Reaper is a therapist too?"

"I am. My name is Azrael, and I'll guide you through your grief."

"Grief?" He puffed out his chest. "I'm not grieving; I'm pissed. I had a plan. I..."

Azrael felt for the guy as his brow crumpled and remorse set in. It happened to them all, this brief bout of clarity before the denial returned.

"Would you care to share your regret?"

His posture deflated. "I never told Elizabeth how I felt."

He wasn't surprised Joey shared so easily. Counseling the dead was what Azrael was created to do, so they almost always opened up immediately. Getting them to accept their lives were over was the hard part. "Who is Elizabeth?"

"My lawyer. I fell in love with her years ago, but I've been so focused on my work, I kept putting off starting a relationship with her." He looked at Azrael, and a tear slid down his cheek. "I'm forty-two. I had all the time in the world."

"You had all the time Fate gave you."

"No." He clenched his jaw and shook his head. "No, I have to see her."

And we're back in denial. The spirit

tried to get away, but Azrael caught him by the waist with his scythe and whisked him into the Underworld, where he couldn't do any damage. A soul left to roam the earth could wreak havoc on the living once he figured out how to manipulate objects. In Purgatory, they were easily subdued when they got ornery.

They arrived in Azrael's office, and the décor morphed into a scene resembling a high-rise office with a white linoleum floor and drab green furniture. A stock ticker hung on the wall, displaying the happenings of the NASDAQ, but Azrael flicked his wrist, making it disappear. Joey would never leave denial if he was constantly watching the stock market. Money didn't exist where he would eventually be headed.

"You're free to roam the premises." Azrael sank into the chair behind his desk and pulled up his calendar. "Your first counseling session begins tomorrow at eleven a.m. in this office. Unless there's anything you want to discuss now, you may go."

"You have to put me back. That's what I want to discuss."

"I'm afraid that's not possible. There's a coffee bar to the right when you exit the building. You'll find other spirits there. The company of others in the same circumstances can be therapeutic."

Joey grunted and stomped out the door.

In the old days, Azrael would attempt to begin counseling the moment the spirit entered Purgatory. Over the ages, he'd learned those in the beginning of denial needed time to sort through their emotions on their own. Tomorrow, after he'd acclimated to the new environment, Joey would be ready to begin the grieving process.

Azrael rolled the tension from his shoulders, his body relaxing as his office returned to its all-black Angel of Death façade.

The biggest regret spirits usually had was not fully experiencing love while they were alive. Azrael would never understand that regret. He had experienced love, and he'd lost her to time. Whoever said, "It's better to have loved and lost than never loved at all," was full of shit.

His mind drifted back to his time with

Nora. Sure, the fifty years he spent with her were the best years of his life, but for an immortal, fifty years was nothing more than a drop of water in a never-ending sea of monotony. It had pained him to watch her grow old and die, and when she passed, she took a piece of him with her, leaving a hole in his heart that would never be filled. No way in hell would he go through that again.

"Good morning." Jessie stood in the doorway looking sheepish and holding two paper cups from the coffee shop. "I brought a peace offering. I hope you're not too angry with me."

He leaned back in his chair and crossed his arms. He should be furious. "You knew it was speed dating night when you convinced me to go."

"Yeah..." She strode into the room,

her heels clicking on the black marble floor, and set one cup of coffee on his desk before perching on the edge and sipping her own drink.

"And Eve and Aphrodite? Even Lucifer? They were in on it too?"

She grinned. "I had to get you back out there, Boss. It's hard to help clients through their grief when you're depressed yourself."

"I'm not depressed." He uncrossed his arms and grabbed the cup she had offered him. He took a sip. The coffee was black and strong, just how he liked it. "I'm not angry either. If I'm being honest, I'll admit I ended up having a good time last night."

Her smile widened. "That's good to hear. You didn't seem interested in any of the potential dates, and you booked it out of there as soon as it ended. I was afraid I'd be facing your wrath this morning."

He chuckled. "You should be, but one of the women did pique my interest. And I succumbed to that one-night stand you prescribed."

"Ha! I knew you got laid. You're positively glowing." She set down her cup and folded her hands in her lap. "Which one? Tell me all about her."

"It was Deirdre, the blonde vampire." His lips curled into a smile of their own volition at the mention of her name.

"The one in hot pink? I have to say, if you were going to choose any of them, I expected you to go for the goth witch with the black lipstick. She seemed more your type."

"She exuded doom and gloom, and I

get enough of that here. There's something about Deirdre. She's undead, but she's so full of life." Was that a flutter in his belly? If so, he needed to squelch that shit before it flitted up to his chest. He'd been relieved when Deirdre had insisted he leave before dawn. Truth be told, after the spell she'd cast on him with her wiles, he'd still be there if she would have asked him to stay. But maybe that wouldn't be such a bad thing...

Jesse arched a brow. "And when are you going to see her again?"

"I'm not. Neither of us is looking for a relationship, so we agreed it would be a one-time thing."

"Uh-huh. I'm not buying what you're selling, Boss. She had an effect on you. I can tell."

Jessie had no idea. "You're right. She did exactly what you wanted her to do. She reminded me how to have fun, and she helped me relieve my stress. Happy?"

"Hmm. If you say so." She rose and took her coffee from the desk. "But if that's all she was to you, why have you added pink to your office decor?" She brushed her hand across a hot pink miniature coffin on the corner of his desk before turning and striding out the door.

Azrael tilted his head and gazed at the casket. About four inches long, it was tapered at the end like a classic Dracula-style coffin but in Deirdre's signature color. That wasn't there before Jessie arrived, was it? Surely she put it on his desk to mess with him.

The counseling center offices were designed to change their décor based on what the soul needed to see. The same was true for the angels who occupied the offices when their clients weren't there. Why on earth would he need a reminder of Deirdre? He already couldn't get the woman off his mind, but that was because she had awakened a sexual desire in him that had been dormant for far too long.

It was purely primal. Nothing more.

As the days passed, however, his thoughts of the vivacious vampire became more insistent. Sure, the memory of their escapade between sheets hardened his dick day and night, but he found himself thinking about more than her hotter-than-hellfire body. Long before they made it to her apartment, they had *fun.* She was adventurous and confident. A light in his world of darkness and grief.

He ventured topside three days in a row, enjoying the buzz of activity rather than avoiding it. He even met a few reapers for dinner one night, something he hadn't done in...well, he couldn't remember how long.

Now, as he stood at the top of the hill in the park, gazing at the moonlit sky above, he smiled. Spinning in a circle to be sure no humans were around, he unfurled his wings and took to the sky. His magic would make him appear as a bird to any wandering eyes, and he swooped over the city, retracing the path he'd taken with Deirdre.

The cool breeze in his feathers and the moon above were glorious, but his flight wasn't nearly as exhilarating as it was with Deirdre in his arms. He lowered to the ground and sat in the swing. She'd asked him to leave that night, even when he'd offered to stay. What made him think she would want to see him again, he wasn't sure, but he had felt a connection with her. She must have felt it too.

He needed to see her again, and he had a feeling he knew exactly where he could find her Wednesday night.

***

Deirdre stood in front of a bookcase, reading the titles of the books, examining the artifacts on the shelves, and looking at anything and everything except the woman sitting in the pale yellow chair. Thick white carpet squished beneath her shoes as she stepped toward an iron mask positioned in a stand at eye level. Reaching out a hand, she brushed her fingers along the rivets protruding from its seams.

"Don't touch that."

She jerked her hand back and turned toward the woman. "Sorry. Is it antique?"

"I've had it for three hundred years." She picked up a pen and a notepad and wrote something on the page.

Deirdre looked at the wall behind an ornately carved oak desk. Dozens of framed certificates filled the space, touting Dr. Laura Monroe's experience. She cast her gaze back to the shelf and picked up a book titled *The Psychology of Vampires.*

"Please put that back and have a

seat, Deirdre. You never know what kind of magic another supe's possessions might contain. You could have cursed yourself."

She returned the book and tentatively sank into the chair. "I doubt you'd keep a cursed artifact on display in your office. You're a therapist."

"Most adults know to keep their hands to themselves."

Deirdre crossed her legs and studied Dr. Monroe. Her dark brown hair was styled into a pixie cut, and a muted shade of peach lipstick complemented her umber skin nicely. After writing something else on her notepad, she smiled sympathetically, showing fang.

"What brings you in for therapy?"

She shrugged. That was the million-dollar question, wasn't it? Why the hell was she here? She didn't have any issues. Her life was one adventure after the next, and now she was in a brand-new city, L fucking A of all places. It was probably the only city in the country more exciting than New Orleans.

"What thoughts were you having when you decided to make an appointment?"

Deirdre inhaled deeply. "I guess I just wanted somebody to talk to. I haven't made any friends here yet."

"I see." Dr. Monroe's pen scratched across the paper.

"What are you writing?" Deirdre leaned forward, trying to make out her upside-down cursive.

"Just taking notes to jog my memory on our next session. What about work colleagues? Do you talk to anyone there?"

"I'm a web designer. I work from my apartment."

"Do you talk to anyone from your former home?"

Deirdre chewed the inside of her cheek. She really did not want to get into this with a stranger, but ever since that smokin' hot dark angel came into her life, talking about how the dead needed therapy, she couldn't shake the idea that it might be good for the undead as well.

"I had a roommate in New Orleans. She married a god and became a goddess herself, so I don't see her much anymore. When you live as long as I...as we...do, people don't stay in your life very long."

Dr. Monroe tilted her head. "The right people do."

She scoffed. "I'm sure Kat will visit me when she can. She's a good friend, but she lives in Seattle now. Everyone else I've ever known can suck it."

The pen made that damn scratching sound on the paper again, and Deirdre lowered her gaze to her lap.

"I'm sensing you have a hard time letting people in. Do you have any idea why that is?"

"Oh, I don't know. Maybe it's because everyone I've ever cared about has either died or left me high and dry."

"Who in particular? Mortals dying is something we vampires have to grow accustomed to, or we'll go insane with grief."

When Deirdre didn't reply, she continued, "You've been undead how long?"

CARRIE PULKINEN

"About two hundred years."

"So you've already grieved the loss of your human family. Who else do you miss?"

"I don't *miss* anyone. The man who turned me promised to make me his mate. Five years and three dozen mistresses later, he took off to France, and I haven't heard from him since."

"Ah. I see. And relationships since then? How have those worked out?"

"I've had plenty of relationships. I haven't found anyone worth keeping around more than a few weeks, but I date. I have fun."

"I never doubted your ability to have fun. Hot pink isn't an easy color to pull off, but you do it splendidly." She jotted down another note. "Have you dated since you arrived in L.A.?"

"I went to speed dating at DeLux Café last week. Does that count?"

"If you believe it does, yes. Did you meet anyone you liked?"

An image of a naked Azrael flashed behind her eyes, and she smiled.

"You did," Dr. Monroe mused.

"I did, but I can't see him again."

"Why not?"

"He was too..." Hot, beautiful, kind, perfect. "He's not my type."

Dr. Monroe inclined her chin, silently urging Deirdre to elaborate, but there was nothing more to say. Azrael had made it clear he wasn't looking for anything more than a fling, as had she. Even if she wanted to see him again—which she did not—he didn't want to see her.

She held the doctor's gaze, refusing to

speak for as long as possible, but when Dr. Monroe didn't waver, Deirdre continued, "I liked him too much. I always end relationships before they can get serious, but with Azrael, I'm afraid I wouldn't want to end it. There was something about him, you know? He was so...introspective. Is that the right word? I don't know, but it felt like he *knew* me even though we'd just met. Like he could see into my soul."

Her brow rose in surprise. "Did you say Azrael? The Angel of Death?"

Deirdre lifted her hands. "I know. He's not the type of man a vampire should get involved with. We did sort of cheat death, after all."

"On the contrary." She set her pad and pen aside. "Deirdre, I sense you have abandonment issues after your sire left you alone."

She laughed cynically. "Ya think?"

"What better man to get involved with than an immortal with a steady job and a reputation for longevity?"

"His *longevity* is a good quality." Another image flashed behind her eyes. He was long, all right. Thick too. *Yum.*

"Our time is up for today." Dr. Monroe rose and motioned toward the door. "Perhaps you should consider seeing him again."

Deirdre stood, shaking her head as she strode toward the exit. "Oh no. That's not happening."

"Not even on the advice of your therapist?"

"I appreciate your expertise in the psychology of vampires, but when it comes to relationships, I know what's best for me. Thanks for listening."

Deirdre made her way out of the building and onto the sidewalk before pausing and curling her hands into fists. She definitely did not need to see Azrael again. What she needed was a new flavor of the month to get her mind off the hotter-than-the-tarpits-of-hell angel, and she knew just where to find one.

Azrael wouldn't be setting foot anywhere near DeLux Café on speed dating night, so that was exactly where she'd be on Wednesday.

CHAPTER SIX

DEIRDRE SHOWED THE bouncer her ID
and headed straight for the red velvet
curtain separating the upstairs mortal
area of DeLux Café from the
underground supernatural level. Like
last week, an explosion of pink and red
hearts decorated the scene, and she
waited in line behind a petite ocelot

shifter to check in for the fun.

"Back for more?" Eve grinned as Deirdre stepped up to the table. "We've got a few repeat customers tonight. Men and women."

Deirdre's pulse sprinted, and she jerked her head toward the men's waiting area. Whether she was excited at the prospect of Azrael being there or horrified, she wasn't sure, but a sigh of relief escaped her lips when he was nowhere to be seen.

She ran her fingertips over the tablecloth and reached for the centerpiece, stopping herself when Eve raised a brow. "I had so much fun last week, I figured why not give it another go?" She took her ballot from the vampire's hand.

Eve winked. "Here's hoping you find

true love tonight."

"Thanks." But no thanks. No way.

She stopped by the bar on her way to her assigned table, and this time she did imbibe the whiskey-laced AB negative the tall, pale, and handsome vampire from New Orleans had raved about last week. Lilith knew she needed it. She had a bad case of the jitters.

Sliding into the seat at table five, she slipped her legs, clad in pink faux leather, beneath the tablecloth and peered down at her black corset. She'd forgotten her pants wouldn't show at this event. Oh well, her shimmery pink eyeshadow should clue the men in that she wasn't there to play out their gothic fantasies. She'd gotten enough of that lifestyle when she was with her sire all those years ago. Tonight, she was here to have fun.

Eve smiled as she tapped the microphone and waited for everyone's attention. As the murmur of the crowd quieted, she spoke, "You all know the rules, so, gentlemen, please approach your assigned starting table and let the games begin!"

Deirdre scanned the men's faces—and bodies—as they filed into the center of the room. She sipped her drink, contemplating which ones had potential. Then her gaze locked on *him,* and she nearly choked on the blood.

Azrael.

She sputtered and wiped her mouth with a napkin. Thankfully, he hadn't seen her yet and missed her reaction. Contemplating a quick escape, she cut her gaze toward the staircase. If she were in a room full of humans, she could use her vampire speed to jet out of there so quickly no one would know what happened to her.

Sadly, every person here was a supe, which meant enhanced eyesight and reflexes. There was no way she could leave now without making a scene. She would have to put on her big girl britches and face the man who made her feel things she swore she'd never feel again. Thankfully, she had time to compose herself before she had to see him. He started three tables away from her.

The first man sat at her table, but she hardly heard a word he said. Azrael didn't seem interested in his first date either. His gaze wandered over the wall behind her, off to the side, and then he met Deirdre's eyes.

His own widened briefly, his nostrils flaring as recognition took hold. The woman he was supposed to be talking to looked at Deirdre, and her gaze bounced between them. Then she smiled and said something that caught Azrael's attention. He looked confused for a moment, but then he nodded and stood.

The buzzer sounded for the men to move, and Azrael's long strides took him past the two men he was supposed to stay behind and straight to Deirdre's table. He pulled out the chair and sank into it, his gaze never straying from hers as the guy who was supposed to see her next tapped him on the shoulder.

"Hey, man. You skipped a few." He was short and slim, like a fae.

"Move to the empty seat." Azrael

cocked his head at her, an amused smile lighting on those full, sexy lips.

"That's not the way this works." Irritation edged his voice.

Azrael turned in his chair and gave the man a look that could have frozen an ice cube in the bowels of Hell. The fae grumbled, but he did as he was told and took the empty seat.

"What are you doing here?" Azrael's voice was unreadable. She couldn't tell if he was irritated she was in Purgatory again, happy to see her, or just plain bemused.

She straightened her spine—not that she could slouch much in a corset, but still—and arched a brow. "Same as last week. I'm looking for a date. The real question is, what are you doing here? You swore you only did this before because you were forced."

Heat sparked in his eyes as his gaze dipped to her cleavage. "I'm also looking for someone."

She sipped her drink. "Seems we both had the same idea."

"It does. Although, if I'm honest, I—"

The buzzer sounded again, but Azrael didn't move. That was just fine with Deirdre because she was dying to know what he had to say.

The man from table four stood next to them. "It's time to rotate."

Azrael barely spared him a glance. "You'll be skipping this one tonight."

"No. You get five minutes. If you want more, you can meet up after."

The angel winked at her, and damn it if a shiver didn't shimmy up her spine.

"I'm not finished here, so you can

either move to the next lady, or we can take this outside."

The man eyed Azrael as if sizing him up and then moved on to table six.

Deirdre grinned. If *she* were being honest, she'd admit his territorial display lit a fire in her core and made her panties wet. "You were saying something about being honest."

He held her gaze, looking well past her eyes and deep into her soul. She could practically feel his wing wrapped around her body as he smoldered at her, and the calming sensation she'd felt while in his arms last week washed over her again. What was it about Death that brought her so much peace?

A look of indecision tightened his features for a moment before he squared his shoulders and nodded in resolve. "I was looking for you."

"Oh." A giggle bubbled up from her throat, and if it were possible for a vampire to blush, she'd have been as red as a boiled crawfish. She needed to respond, but his words had scattered her thoughts like billiard balls.

He cleared his throat. "I'm surprised to see you in all black. Going goth tonight?"

How did he do that? He'd sensed her unease and changed the subject, giving her mind time to catch up to what was happening.

"Not hardly." She slid her leg out from beneath the table to show her pink pants.

He flashed an appreciative grin. "That's my girl."

"*Your* girl?" Damn him for making her

stomach flutter.

His eyes widened like he hadn't meant to say it. "I mean, that's how I've imagined you over the week."

"You've been imagining me?"

He smoldered at her again, leaning forward and resting his arms on the table. "What if I have?"

"I can live with that." She had imagined him quite a few times over the week as well, though clothing was rarely involved in her daydreams. "The woman you sat with first...what did she say to you?"

He chuckled. "She said I was obviously smitten with you, so I shouldn't waste anyone's time by playing this game."

"And here you are, pissing off all the guys who want a chance with me."

"Would they have a chance with you?"

"Not while you're around." What in Lilith's name was she doing? Flirting with Death was not on her agenda tonight, but she couldn't deny her attraction to this man. One more night wrapped in the wings of an angel wouldn't hurt, would it?

Yes. Yes, it would. She'd just listed all the reasons she couldn't see him anymore at her session with Dr. Monroe. Then again, the good doctor's rebuttal was quite convincing. Azrael was immortal, so she'd never lose him to time. He'd had a steady job for millennia, and that reputation for longevity? Out of all the denizens of the Underworld, he had never been known as a player.

Yes, she'd asked around. She couldn't

help herself. Don't judge.

The buzzer sounded again, and a demon as tall and muscular as Azrael approached their table. "Move it along, Az. She's mine now."

Azrael's brow slammed down over his eyes, and he shot to his feet to face the demon. "I'm not done talking to her."

At least he didn't claim she belonged to him. That might've been a total turn off...or maybe a turn *on*. *Gah!* Simply being near him had her thoughts as twisted as a contortionist eating a jumbo pretzel.

Screw it. She wanted him. He wanted her. There was no sense in fighting a desire this strong. She downed the rest of her drink and rose, taking Azrael by the arm. "It's obvious we're only interested in each other. I think we should bow out of the game, don't you, *cher*?"

He grunted, eyeing the demon like he was ready to fight to the death for her. *So fucking hot.* Sliding his arm around her back, he tugged her to his side and led her to the stairs. As they ascended the steps toward the mortal level, he tucked his wings behind his back, and they disappeared. She rested her hand between his shoulder blades, and sure enough, they were gone.

Deirdre bit her bottom lip but released it as they entered the top level so she didn't flash fang. He could have retracted his wings during their sexy times last week, but he'd chosen not to. He'd let her experience his full self on their first encounter. That said something. She didn't care to contemplate exactly what, mostly because her thoughts drifted to a word that started with F and ended with A-T-E.

She used to believe in soulmates. Her jackass sire, Beau, had convinced her he was hers, but that was bullshit. She gazed at Azrael's profile as they exited the café. His strong jaw and sharp cheekbones exuded sexy masculinity. The physical attraction she felt was a no-brainer, but there was something more. Something deeper.

Devil damn her, but she wanted to explore it. She wanted to *know* him, inside and out. In the words of her absolute favorite singer, Taylor Swift, it could either last forever, or it could go down in a ball of flames hotter than the fires of Hell itself. Only time would tell, and they had all the time in the world.

***

Azrael led Deirdre onto the sidewalk and across the intersection, away from the café. Her being here tonight was a sign. It had to be. Throughout the week, more and more pink had found its way into his office décor. None of it was his doing. Well, not his conscious doing anyway, but when his black marble floor changed to rose quartz, he knew he would do whatever it took to see her again.

Showing up at her apartment unannounced would have been majorly creepy, but that would've been his next step if he hadn't seen her at DeLux tonight. But she *was* at DeLux, right where he thought she'd be.

Now, as they strode side by side down

the sidewalk, he needed to say something, but simply being near her was enough for the moment. She had told him to leave last week when he'd offered to stay. Perhaps she left the café with him tonight to end the confrontation with the demon and nothing more.

He stopped when they reached the end of the next block and turned to her. "Deirdre..."

She placed her finger against his lips, stopping his words. "Have you had dinner? Do you want to grab a bite to eat?"

Her talk of biting and eating had his thoughts drifting to all the things he'd like to do to her once he got her alone. *C'mon, Az,* he chided himself. *Drag your mind out of the gutter.* "Do you mean food?"

"Unless you drink blood, in which case..." She licked her lips. "Never mind."

"No, food works." Food would require conversation, and that was a good thing. If he went home with her now, they'd have a repeat of last week, and he wanted to see if they could be anything more. "Do you...eat?"

She shrugged. "Sure. Food has no nutritional value for me, but I enjoy a rare steak every now and then. Sausage too." She winked and dropped her gaze to his pants. "But maybe I can have that for dessert."

His cock twitched at the seductive way she spoke. Damn, this woman lit his soul on fire. "I know just the place. It's actually near your apartment."

"Already planning the after party as well?" she purred. "I like the way you think."

They definitely needed to start their second date in a very public place. Was it getting hot outside, or was the heat radiating through his veins simply from being in her presence?

"Do you want me to call an Uber?" she asked. "I left my car at home tonight."

"How about we fly?"

She grinned. "Even better."

They slipped into the alley between two buildings, but as he wrapped his arms around her from behind, she spun and planted her lips on his. He returned the kiss, holding her tight to his body and memorizing the way her delicious curves felt against him.

As the kiss slowed, she leaned back and rested her hands on his shoulders. "Just wanted to get that out of the way so we both know where we stand. We want each other's bodies. Now, let's go get to know each other's minds."

He adjusted his now fully hard dick and checked the alley entrance to be sure no mortals were around before unfurling his wings, wrapping his arms around her, and taking to the sky. They shot straight up, high enough that, to the people below, they would look like nothing more than a bird. Of course, his magic helped with that illusion, but Deirdre's bright pink pants could draw unwanted attention if they flew too low.

Once again, she held her arms out to her sides, completely unafraid of the heights at which they soared. "I think this has become my favorite mode of transportation."

"I'm glad you enjoy it. I like it too." In fact, he enjoyed it too much. From the moment his Nora crossed over to the spirit realm, he swore he would never open his heart to another again. Yet here he was, doing just that.

Could the Angel of Death find forever happiness with the undead? One way or another, he intended to find out.

He flew her across town to the Smoke and Embers Steakhouse, and thankfully the place was still in operation. Before he met Deirdre, it had been years...no, decades...since he'd ventured topside to have a meal. In fact, the closest he'd been to the mortal realm in forty years—aside from his visits to the souls he had to reap—was the Underworld side of

DeLux Café.

Maybe the Angel of Death really did need to get a life.

And he held the start of a potential new one in his arms. After landing in the alley, he hid his wings and offered Deirdre his arm. She took it without hesitation and strolled with him to the restaurant entrance.

"Welcome." The host, a man in his early twenties with slick black hair and green eyes, regarded them as if he were bored. "What's the name on the reservation?"

"We don't have one," Azrael replied.

"Mm." He pursed his lips and looked at them like they were naughty children. "We're a reservation-only establishment. I have an opening next Tuesday at six."

They didn't require reservations the

last time he was here, though he couldn't tell the condescending bastard about his visit forty-some-odd years ago. "I see three empty tables right over there."

The host didn't bother turning around to look. "That section is closed."

Azrael's jaw tightened with an audible click. How hard would it be to seat them at a table? No one else was waiting for one. This, right here, was why he preferred to only deal with the dead. The living were so self-absorbed. "Look," he started to argue, but Deirdre patted his bicep and stepped toward the host.

She linked her arm around the man's and touched his shoulder as she whispered something in his ear. Then, she tugged something out of her pocket and passed it to him.

"Right this way." He smiled and seated them in a cozy nook in the back corner of the dining room.

"What did you say to him?" Azrael asked after the man handed them menus and walked away.

Deirdre laughed. "It's not what I said; it's how much I tipped. This section isn't closed, but a host isn't about to seat someone without a reservation for free."

"Interesting." He had a lot to learn about society today. "Do you drink wine?"

"Only when my usual isn't available." She winked, and his stomach fluttered. "Red, please."

"Of course."

When the server arrived, Azrael ordered a bottle of Cabernet Sauvignon.

"What's good here?" Deirdre looked at

her menu, stealing a glance at Azrael as she awaited his answer.

To say he was smitten was an understatement. Her blonde hair cascaded to her shoulders, and her shimmery eyeshadow perfectly accented her sky-blue irises. She looked good in black. Delectable, actually. Hell, she'd look good in Charon's dusty old robes, as long as she only had eyes for Azrael.

She arched a brow when he didn't reply.

He cleared his throat. "Everything. If you're going for rare, the prime rib is excellent. Or...it was forty years ago." He scanned the selection of steaks, deciding on the New York strip for himself.

"Perfect." She folded her menu on the table. "Tell me about Azrael, the Angel of Death."

"What would you like to know?"

"Everything. Let's start with an easy one. How old are you?"

He chuckled and laid his menu next to hers. That one wasn't as easy as she thought. "I honestly don't know."

"As old as the Underworld itself?"

"Older."

She let out a low whistle. "And here I am only two hundred thirty-six. Talk about robbing the cradle." Her smile lit up her entire face. "Were you always a death angel?"

"It's what I was created for: escorting souls to the spirit realm."

The server arrived, and they placed their orders. "And when I say rare," Deirdre said, "I mean slap it on the grill for five seconds and plop it on the plate. I like it bloody as hell."

"I'll let the chef know." The server took the menus and scurried off to the kitchen.

Deirdre sipped her wine before resting her elbow on the table, her chin in her hand. "Now for the ten-million-dollar question. Have you always been single?"

His brow rose as he looked into her eyes. He'd heard from the other angels, who dated much more often than he did, that talking about exes early in a relationship was a red flag. He didn't want to give her any reason to end this thing before it could begin, but she *had* asked. The least he could do was be honest. "No."

She blinked. "No? That's all you have to say about it?"

"Do you want to hear about my past

relationship?"

"I wouldn't have asked if I didn't...wait. Did you say relation*ship*? As in singular? Like you've only ever had one?"

"I did."

"C'mon. A smokin' hot angel like yourself has only ever dated one chick? I find that hard to believe... Unless there's something wrong with you. Is there something wrong with you? Please tell me you don't still live with your mother."

Azrael flashed an amused grin. Was that nervousness he detected in her tone? Why did he find it so endearing?

"I've *dated* several people. As you learned last week, I do have some experience."

"Hell yeah, you do." She took another sip of wine, her shoulders shuddering as if the memory thrilled her.

"I've only had a *relationship* with one. Her name was Nora."

"Tell me about her."

He closed his eyes for a long blink, expecting the familiar emptiness to expand his chest, but he merely felt a slight twinge of discomfort. "She was human. Everyone said I was crazy for falling in love with a mortal. They were right, but I couldn't help it."

"The heart wants what the heart wants."

"Very true."

"What happened to her?"

He smiled sadly. "She loved me, but she wanted nothing to do with the Underworld. I can't blame her; it looked very different back then."

Deirdre cocked her head, her brow

furrowing in a most adorable way.

"It was all fire and brimstone. These days, it's much more refined."

"Interesting. You'll have to give me a tour someday. The closest I've been is the café. Anyway, did you move topside?"

"I split my time. My job is in Purgatory, so I couldn't move to Earth. It worked for us, but she refused any means of becoming immortal. She grew old and died. I reaped her soul and counseled her through her grief, which was the most difficult thing I've ever done."

"I can imagine. You couldn't have assigned another angel to take care of her spirit?"

He shook his head. "What kind of partner would I have been if I abandoned her when she needed my help?"

"Good point." She reached across the table and rested her hand on top of his. Her skin was cool, and the gesture brought him comfort he hadn't expected. "Do you ever go visit her in the spirit realm?"

"Dark angels are forbidden from entering that realm."

Deirdre grimaced. "So you had to lose her twice. I'm so sorry. That must have been hard."

She had no idea how difficult it had been, but... "It was a long time ago, and I grieved my loss properly. Let's not dwell on it."

She smiled softly, brushing her thumb across the back of his hand. "Thanks for sharing."

"I'll tell you anything you want to

know." The words surprised him. He meant it. The only person he shared anything about himself with was Jessie, yet he would answer any question Deirdre asked of him.

He laced his fingers through hers. "Your turn. Have you had any long-term relationships?"

She slipped from his grasp and pressed her lips together, smoothing her napkin in her lap. "It's in the past. Let's leave it there."

"You can talk to me if you're hurting."

She scoffed and lifted her gaze to his eyes. "I'm not."

"Will you tell me how you became a vampire?"

She screwed her mouth over to the side, her gaze becoming distant. Azrael could only imagine what she must have gone through to make her avoid her past like this.

The server arrived with their food, and Deirdre's tense posture relaxed. "This looks amazing." She picked up her silverware, cutting into her steak immediately and shoving a large piece into her mouth.

Azrael could take a hint. He'd drop the subject for now.

They made small talk over dinner, Deirdre telling him about her undead life and all her adventures, while carefully avoiding anything that happened when she was human. She knew how to have fun. Maybe too much fun. As exciting as her second life sounded, Azrael was a trained therapist. She couldn't hide her repressed sadness from him. She was compensating for a loss she refused to acknowledge, and that made her all the more intriguing.

As they ate, her closed-off demeanor shifted, the bubbly, flirtatious woman who'd originally caught his eye resurfacing.

He wanted to know both sides of Deirdre. The light and the dark.

CHAPTER SEVEN

AZRAEL SAW DEIRDRE several times a week over the next month, their dates bringing them closer together, their time between the sheets getting hotter with each passing day. She was still guarded. Every time he tried to steer the conversation toward her life as a human or her transition to becoming a vampire, she'd either change the subject or distract him.

She was *so* good at distracting him.

His patience with the living was thin at best, but Deirdre was different. *He* was different with her, and while the Angel of Death was dying to know her story, he could wait. She would open up eventually. In the meantime, he could enjoy her company.

Now, as he lay on the ground beneath the H of the hillside Hollywood sign, his wings stretched out beneath him, Deirdre lying by his side, he couldn't recall a time he'd ever been more content. A cool fall breeze wafted the sweet, spicy scent of white ginger flowers to his senses, and Deirdre's hand on his chest provided a comfort he hadn't realized he was missing.

"The stars used to be so much brighter." Her voice roused him from his thoughts.

He turned his head toward her and kissed her cheek. "The marvels of human ingenuity have taken away some of Earth's beauty."

"Do you ever wish things could go back to the way they used to be before the internet, television...electricity?"

"Times were simpler in the past, but progress is inevitable. There's no sense dwelling on the way things used to be." That was a lesson he'd been teaching himself over the past month. He'd sworn off love after Nora passed, afraid his heart wouldn't survive a second break, but Deirdre... She was worth the risk.

Azrael had spent the past few decades feeling like Death warmed over.

Deirdre may have been undead, but she made him feel more alive than he'd ever felt. She was also immortal, which meant—as long as she didn't get staked—she could live forever...with him. Heat spread through his chest at the thought.

"What do you think the world will be like in another hundred years?" she asked.

"We'll have to wait and see."

She rolled toward him, resting her chin on his chest. "Let's come here one hundred years from today and have this conversation again." Her smile brightened her eyes. "I can't even begin to imagine what things will be like."

He tucked her hair behind her ear, running his fingers through the silky strands, and his heart swelled with joy that she suggested they would still be together then. "Deal."

Her brow rose as if she suddenly realized the implications of what she said. Her lips parted, and she laid her head on his shoulder, snuggling closer to him. He curled his wing around her protectively...not that there was anything to protect her from up here on the side of the hill. The place was fenced off, no one allowed to venture into the area.

She ran her fingers down the underside of his feathers, and a warm shiver ran up his spine. "I love it when you do this," she said.

"Do what?"

"Wrap your wing around me. It makes me feel safe, cared for."

He curled his other wing around her

too. "I care for you more than you know."

"Let's go to your place tonight. I want to see the Underworld."

He inhaled deeply. All their dates thus far had ended at her apartment. The reasons were twofold: they'd spent all their time together topside, and he hadn't brought a woman to his home since Nora passed.

But he hadn't felt this way about anyone before. "I'll give you the grand tour."

She giggled and sat up. "Let's go now. I've never been at Death's doorstep before..." She ran a finger down his chest. "Or in his bed."

They stood and assumed the position he'd grown fond of: her back pressed against his front, his arms wrapped tightly around her. Unfurling his wings, he prepared to take flight, but a flashlight beam nearly blinded him.

"Hey! You can't be up here." A security guard stomped toward them.

"Whoops," Deirdre said.

Azrael flapped his wings, taking to the sky.

"Holy shit!" The guard dropped his flashlight and scrambled to pick it up.

"Fuck. He saw my wings." He hadn't activated his magic quickly enough, not that his bird guise would have worked at such close range. "Lucifer's going to be pissed."

"I can make him forget," Deirdre said. "Take us back to the ground."

He did as she asked, releasing her as their feet hit the grass. Tucking his wings against his back, he crossed his arms, his muscles tense as she slunk toward the shaking man.

"Wha...what are you?" he stuttered.

"Just a couple of supes enjoying the view," she purred. "There's no harm in that."

His eyes glazed over. "There's no harm in that."

Azrael raised his brow. He'd never witnessed Deirdre using her vampire glamour, and it was hotter than hellfire. *Damn.*

"In fact..." She rested a hand on the man's shoulder. "You won't even remember we were here."

He shook his head. "I won't remember."

Deirdre looked at Azrael over her shoulder. "Do you mind if I have a snack, *cher*? I'm famished."

"Be my guest."

She sank her fangs into the man's neck, and his eyes rolled back like he enjoyed being her meal. This was also the first time Azrael had seen her drink blood straight from the source.

He tensed, a flush of desire setting his blood on fire. *Holy fuck, that's hot.*

When she finished, she licked the man's neck, sealing the wounds. "You saw nothing."

She turned and strutted toward Azrael, her tongue slipping out to catch a drop of blood on the corner of her mouth.

His own blood rushed to his groin, hardening his dick in an instant. "Have you ever used your glamour on me?"

She lifted one shoulder dismissively. "I tried once, just to see. It didn't work."

He licked his lips and swept his gaze

down her gloriously curvy body. "Why have you never bitten me?"

A seductive smile curved her pink lips. "You've never asked me to. I don't make a habit of getting my sustenance from the people I care about."

He chuckled. "So you do care about me."

"More than I ever thought possible."

He adjusted his dick through his pants.

"We better get you home so I can take care of that for you." She palmed his groin and squeezed, sending a jolt of electricity straight to his core. "And I don't want to have to glamour the rent-a-cop again. It's not good for the weak human brain. Shall we?"

She turned around, and he held her from behind, flying home as fast as his wings would take them. As they reached the Underworld entrance and stepped inside, her breath caught. "This is not how I imagined it at all."

He moved behind her, massaging her shoulders as he pressed a kiss to her neck. "I know I promised you a tour, but we're going to save that for later."

Goosebumps rose on her skin, and her words came out as a whisper, "Good idea."

Cradling her in his arms, he flew her to his home. Tabitha meowed as they stepped inside, and she rubbed against Deirdre's leg.

"Well, hello there, beautiful." She kneeled to pet her. "What's your name?"

"That's Tabitha." He strode into the kitchen and cracked a window, and his cat darted outside.

"She's cute."

"There's a hellhound a block over she likes to play with. She'll be gone for a while." He clutched her hip, pulling her to his body.

"Privacy is good." She laced her fingers behind his neck. "Especially for all the things I have planned for you."

"Hmm..." He ran his hands up and down her sides. He'd long since memorized the way she felt beneath his touch, and he couldn't get enough of her. "My house, *my* plans." He scooped her into his arms and carried her to his bedroom.

"You really like the color black, don't you?" she asked as he set her feet on the floor. "Is your office like this too?"

He chuckled. If she could only see his office now. "It changes décor to match what the client needs. When I'm alone, it appears how I need it."

"So all black then?" She turned in a circle, taking in her surroundings. Thankfully, his home didn't change to match his needs.

"Lately, a few pink things have been popping up."

"Nice. Pink's my favorite color."

"Which is exactly why it's happening. I need you in my life, Deirdre. You've changed me, shown me how to live again."

Her lips parted on a quick breath, her gaze locking with his. When she closed her mouth and swallowed hard, his stomach sank. Had he misread the signs? Said too much too soon?

"Is that your scythe?" She pointed to where it stood against the wall.

Yep. Too much too soon. *Good going, Az. Way to scare off the one good thing in your eternal life.* "Yes, that's Severus."

She laughed, unbelieving. "You named your scythe after a children's book character?"

"I have no idea what you're referring to."

"We have to get you caught up on pop culture. It's an icon. There are movies, even a theme park."

While he read mostly classics—and he had read them all—if she wanted to experience "pop culture" with him, he would be happy to oblige. "Severus was forged millennia before the first theme park came into existence. I assure you he was not named after anything. He severs souls; thus, I call him Severus."

"He's beautiful." She moved toward

the scythe, but he caught her by the hand.

"Don't touch it. Mere contact with the blade severs the soul from the body. It requires no magic from the wielder."

She titled her head at it, splaying her fingers before clutching them into fists. "But I'm a vampire. Surely it wouldn't affect me."

"I'm positive it would." He and Lucifer himself were the only beings immune to the celestial metal.

She nodded, casting her gaze to the floor for a moment before looking into his eyes. "Azrael..." She moved toward him and placed a soft kiss on his cheek. "We've been dating a month, and this is the point where I normally end a relationship."

Oh, hell. He hadn't just misread the

signs; apparently, they were written in a completely different language. One he didn't understand. "I see."

She cupped his face in her hand. "But I don't want to end it with you. For the first time in more than two hundred years, I'm not afraid. You've changed me too."

Cool relief flooded his veins, and joy warmed his chest. Wrapping his arms around her waist, he pulled her close. "I'm so glad we're on the same page."

"So am I." She crushed her mouth to his, brushing her tongue against his before nipping at his bottom lip.

As her fangs softly scraped his skin, his dick strained against the fabric of his jeans. "I liked watching you feed tonight," he said against her mouth.

"Yeah?" She yanked his shirt up over

his head—having mastered the break-away wing flap long ago—and tossed it aside. "Did it turn you on?"

He removed her shirt and unhooked her bra with a twist of his fingers. "It was hot as fuck."

The coolness of her skin against his tamed a fever he never knew he had, and as she unzipped his jeans and gripped his cock, a deep moan rumbled in his chest. Dropping to her knees, she tugged the garments down and licked him from base to tip. The sensation made him gasp, and as she looked up at him, she took his length into her mouth and sucked him.

Sweet Cerberus, the woman was good at that. She cupped his balls in her hand and circled his tip with her tongue before taking him in again and sucking *hard.* Her teeth grazed his sensitive flesh, and his body shuddered.

He allowed himself to enjoy it for another moment before twisting his fingers in her hair and gently tugging her glorious lips away from his cock. "My turn."

She rose to her feet, and he picked her up before tossing her onto his bed. "Satin sheets." She ran her hands over the fabric. "I like."

He kicked his shoes and jeans aside before unbuttoning her pants. She lifted her hips, allowing him to remove the rest of her clothes, and she moved to the center of the mattress. Azrael stood at the foot of the bed, admiring her beauty. Her blonde hair spilled out around her shoulders, and his fingers twitched with the urge to caress every inch of her fair skin. She was his opposite in every way. A light in his dark world.

"Are you going to stand there all night, or are you going to make me come?"

"Oh, you'll come, sweetheart. Again and again." He lay on top of her, his wings folded against his back as he kissed her.

She ran her fingers over his feathers, and fire shot through his veins. She knew exactly where to touch, how much pressure was enough to make his skin turn to gooseflesh. He wouldn't be surprised if she could make him come from simply stroking his wings.

Moving down her body, he kissed, licked, and nipped, leaving not a single inch of flesh untouched. She moaned as he sucked a nipple into his mouth, and as he moved down to her stomach, she tangled her fingers in his hair.

He circled his tongue around her navel before trailing it down to her hairline. She gasped as he blew a breath over her clit, exhaling slowly when he pressed his lips to her inner thigh.

"Please, Azrael," she whispered softly as he blew another warm breath.

"What do you want me to do?" He kissed her other thigh.

"Lick me. Make me come and then fuck me so hard I can't walk after."

"My pleasure."

He flicked out his tongue, bathing her sensitive nub in wet heat, and she let out an erotic moan that rivaled the most experienced succubus. She clutched the sheets as he licked her, and when he gently sucked her clit between his lips, brushing it with his tongue, she cried out his name.

Never in a million years could he have imagined pleasing another would give *him* so much pleasure. His cock ached with the need to fill her, and he reached down to stroke it as he continued his pursuit with his tongue.

"It's so fucking hot when you touch yourself." Deirdre looked at him through hooded eyes.

A growl rumbled up from his chest, and he released his dick to slide his fingers inside her. She dropped her head back on the pillow, panting as he turned his hand over to reach her sweet spot. He stroked the sensitive area inside her, moving his fingers back and forth as his tongue caressed her clit.

"Oh my god, Azrael!" Her hips bucked

beneath him, her body nearly convulsing with her orgasm. "Holy fuck, yes!"

The sound of her coming, of his name on her lips in the throes of ecstasy, thrilled him to no end. He softened his motions, bringing her down slowly before increasing the pressure and taking her up again. Three orgasms later, she begged him to fill her.

With a swift thrust of his hips, they joined together as one. He lay on top of her, moving in and out slowly, relishing the feel of her wrapped around him, squeezing him.

"Harder, Azrael," she rasped into his ear.

His wings unfurled across the bed, and he hooked his arms behind her shoulders, thrusting firmly, his movements growing faster as the orgasm coiled in his core. "Bite me, Deirdre."

"Are you sure?" she panted.

"Yes. Fucking bite me. Drink from me." He tucked his wings, rolling onto his back, never breaking their union.

She worked her hips as she lay her chest on his, sliding up and down his cock and pressing her fangs against his neck. She hesitated, but when he didn't waver, she bit.

Every nerve in his body went on rapid fire when her teeth pierced his flesh, and as she covered the wound with her mouth and sucked, he lost control. His orgasm exploded through his body, burning him from the inside out, sending him to heaven and back to Purgatory again. Gripping her hips, he pumped his own, riding the wave until she released his neck and came again.

"Holy fuck." She stilled and licked his wound. "Was that as good for you as it was for me?"

"You have no idea." He leaned up to spread his wings, and she rolled off him, snuggling into his side.

They lay there, wrapped in each other's arms, basking in the afterglow. Deirdre was the one. He had no doubt in his mind Fate had sent her to him right when he needed her, and he would do everything in his power to make her his mate. After a while, Azrael closed his eyes and began to doze.

"I was twenty-two when I was turned." Deirdre's soft whisper roused him from sleep. She didn't lift her head from his shoulder. "His name was Beau, and he swore we were soulmates. He abandoned me five years later, and that's all I care to say about it."

He kissed her forehead. "Thank you for sharing."

CHAPTER EIGHT

A PAIR OF warm lips on Deirdre's forehead awakened her from slumber. She kept her eyes closed as Azrael traced his fingers across her collarbone before running the back of his hand down her cheek. "Be careful, reaper." She smiled. "A girl could get used to this."

"I hope you do." He pressed his lips to

hers.

Sweet Lilith, how she loved his warmth. As a vampire, she'd grown accustomed to being cold as a corpse. Azrael was warmer than any man she'd ever been with, and she never imagined how much it would appeal to her. How everything about him would be so...wonderful. He was kind, sweet, tough when he needed to be, but he was also in touch with his own emotions—and hers—which was hella sexy in a man. She fluttered her lids open and found him smiling at her.

"Good morning, beautiful."

"Morning?" She stretched her arms over her head. "I think you mean night."

"It's eight a.m. We've been asleep for hours."

"No way." He had to be joking. "I

never fall asleep while the moon is still out. Vampires sleep in the daylight hours."

"The sun doesn't shine in Purgatory." He rubbed his hand over the sexy scruff that had formed on his chin. "It must've messed with your internal clock."

Azrael rose, and she blinked as she took in his fully clothed form. "Are you going somewhere?"

He flashed a heart-melting smile. "I've already been. You'll have to stay in the Underworld until darkness falls topside, so I brought you some supplies." He set a fabric bag on the bed and began pulling out items as he spoke. "A laptop in case you need to get some work done. I assume you have everything saved to the cloud?"

She sat up, letting the satin sheets

fall away from her body, grinning as his gaze dipped to her breasts. "Of course."

"I also got you a bottle of blood. As much as I enjoyed you using me as a snack last night, we better not flood your system with angel blood. I don't know what effect it might have until you get used to it."

"Aw, but you make such a tasty snack. Sexy too." She laughed. "But I suppose you're right. You're my first angel, so we better be sure I don't sprout wings before we try that again. Though it would be absolutely fabulous if I did."

"I have a soul to reap and a few therapy sessions to run this morning, but I've cleared my schedule for the afternoon. When I'm finished, I'll give you that grand tour I promised."

"Sounds wonderful. Mind if I use your

shower?"

"Make yourself at home." He strode to the corner of the bedroom and took his scythe from its stand.

"It's such a beautiful instrument." Deirdre stood, her fingers twitching with the urge to touch it. To just run her hand along the dull side of the blade one time. It was designed to sever souls from the living. She was undead, which was entirely different. She could get run over by a Mac truck, and as long as it didn't pierce her heart or behead her, she'd recover. Surely a piece of metal wouldn't hurt her.

"Beautiful and deadly." He held the scythe away from his body to lean in for a kiss. "I'll see you soon. Tabitha will keep you company."

The cat jumped onto the bed and

meowed, and Deirdre scooped her into her arms. Azrael smiled, and as he turned to leave, she couldn't fight the temptation. Reaching out her left hand, she brushed her fingers across his blade. Tabitha screeched and scrambled from her arms, falling to the floor with a *thud.*

Azrael spun around, his mouth falling slack. His eyes widened, and Deirdre followed his gaze to the bed behind her. There on the mattress lay her naked body, her expression frozen in a look of shock.

That one quick touch of Azrael's scythe sent her from undead to really dead in half a second flat. *Oh, shit.*

"Look at that. You were right." A maniacal laugh bubbled from her throat, and she slapped her hand over her mouth. Tears welled in her eyes, which was odd as all get-out. Who knew ghosts had bodily fluids?

Azrael sighed. "Yet you didn't believe me."

"My mother warned me I needed to keep my hands to myself. That's a lesson I never learned." A sob lodged in her throat. This could not be happening. She was a vampire, for Lilith's sake. She couldn't die from simply touching a magical blade.

"That's the first time you've ever mentioned your life before you became a vampire." His expression softened as he moved toward her body.

"Why don't you sound the slightest bit concerned? I'm a fucking ghost. I need my body back. I've got things to do. There's more fun to be had." Wait. He said his scythe severed the soul from the body. Maybe she wasn't actually dead yet. Maybe...

She turned around and fell backward onto her corpse, hoping to sink inside and be whole again. But as her spirit touched her flesh, an electric shock ricocheted through her soul. Her limbs shook. She bit her tongue so hard, she would have tasted blood if she had any. It seemed spirits didn't have bodily fluids after all.

She jerked away, rolling onto the mattress and scooting to the opposite edge of the bed. "Devil dammit, that hurt!"

"Once the soul is severed, the body rejects any attempts for rejoining by the spirit." Azrael sat on the bed next to her and stroked his fingers down her ghostly cheek. He still held his damn scythe in his other hand.

More phantom tears gathered in her eyes. "That thing is dangerous. You shouldn't carry it around in the open."

He chuckled. "We're not in the open, and I told you not to touch it, warned you what it would do."

"So that's it then? Here lies Deirdre, dead because she couldn't keep her hands to herself?"

An amused grin tilted his lips.

"Is this funny to you?"

He forced a concerned expression and stood. "No, of course not. Come on. Let's put you back together." He held out his hand.

"You can do that?"

"On occasion, Death gives a second chance. But only when the body isn't damaged, and it wasn't the person's time to go. It's not common knowledge, so don't tell anyone. If word got out, every spirit who crossed through Purgatory would be begging me to return them to life."

Deirdre drew an X over her heart. "I'll take it to the grave."

"That's a place you'll never have to go as long as I'm around. Come."

She accepted his hand and rose, allowing him to guide her around the bed to her corpse. "It's not going to electrocute me again, is it?"

"You'll feel a snap when your soul connects. No one has mentioned pain."

"How many times have you done this?"

He pursed his lips, his brow scrunching. "I don't know. More than a few. New reapers make mistakes and often need help."

"So you know what you're doing?" She shook her head. "Of course you do. You're *the* Angel of Death. I trust you."

He arched a brow. "Do you?"

She looked into his soulful dark brown eyes, and her answer came without hesitation, "I do." *Huh. Imagine that.* Deirdre had spent two centuries building a fortress around her heart, and this dark angel had penetrated it in one month. She did trust him...with every fiber of her being...and if he said he could put her back together, she believed him.

"Let's do this thing. Looking at my own corpse is creeping me out."

Azrael held his scythe toward her, and she instinctively jumped away. That thing had done enough damage.

"You'll need to hold my blade and lay back into your body."

She eyed the scythe skeptically. Yes, she trusted Azrael, but... "Are you sure it's not going to obliterate me? I've seen the TV show *Lucifer*, and 'Azrael's blade' is more than deadly."

He grunted. "Then you also know they portrayed me as a girl. That show is fiction. This is real, and we have a limited time to make you whole before your body will no longer accept your spirit."

"How limited?"

"For the living, it's seventy-two hours. You'll be my first vampire reanimation."

"Okay..." She took a deep breath and clutched the dull side of the blade. Its magic buzzed up her arm before spreading through her entire spirit form like a vibrator on overdrive. Could ghosts have orgasms? That was a question for another day. She didn't plan to be a ghost any longer than she had to.

Azrael moved his scythe, guiding her to her body, and she lay down, her spirit sinking into her corpse. No electric shock. That was good.

"When you let go, you should feel the snap of your soul merging with your body. As soon as you're ready, go for it."

Deirdre released her hold, but she did not feel the snap. Instead, a hundred thousand volts of electricity rocketed through her spirit. Her body rejected her, and her ghostly form flew across the room, slamming into the wall with a *smack*. She sank to the floor and rubbed her head.

"What the hell, man?" If she wasn't already as dead as a door knocker, surely she'd be six feet under after that ordeal.

Azrael's dark brow slammed down over his eyes as he looked from Deirdre's ghost to her body. "I don't understand. That should have worked."

"Yeah, well, it didn't." Deirdre stood and walked tentatively toward the bed. "What went wrong? Is it already too late?"

"I have no idea what went wrong, but it can't possibly be too late. It's been less than ten minutes." Azrael ran his hand down her body's face, closing her eyelids.

A cold shiver crawled up her ghostly spine. Closing her lids felt so...final. "You said I would be your first vampire reanimation. Maybe it's not even possible. Maybe, because I cheated death the first time around, I'm past due, and Lucifer is calling me home."

His hands curled into fists. "Lucifer is not... It *is* possible, and I'm going to fix you."

"How do you know it's possible?"

"Because it has to be." He clutched her shoulders, but she didn't feel the usual warmth of his skin. All she felt was pressure. "I can't lose you, Deirdre. I *won't* lose you. Let me try again."

Her spirit still felt like chicken fricassee, but her heart...or, rather, the sensation of her ghostly heart...swelled with hope. "Do you promise I'm not going to get electrocuted?"

Azrael blew out a hard breath through his nose. "I can't promise that.

Spirits aren't supposed to feel pain at all."

"Fang-fucking-tastic. I'm the anomaly. What are you going to do differently?" Because she could not stand another round in the electric chair.

"Perhaps I didn't instill enough magic into the blade. I'll give it more this time."

"You said the wielder didn't have to use magic."

"For severing souls, we don't. Reanimation is a different story. We have to use our angelic abilities to reverse the scythe's magic."

"You better give it all you've got." Deirdre reached for the blade, and the vibrating power intensified until her entire being shook.

He guided her into her body once

more, and she held her ghostly breath, tensing her form as she awaited the shock. She released the blade.

"Hey, I think it might be work—" The jolt rocketed her into the ceiling. She hit the surface with a *thwack* and plopped onto the bed before scrambling away from her body. "Never mind."

Azrael ground his teeth, working his jaw from side to side. "Something is wrong."

"You think?" Deirdre rolled her neck and shook her arms to chase away the Kentucky fried sensation.

Azrael pulled out his phone and typed on the screen before closing his eyes and doing *something* with his magic. A pulse went through her form, and the panic coursing through her—well, she didn't have veins, so what was it coursing through? Anyway, it subsided.

"What did you just do?"

He returned the phone to his pocket. "I cleared my schedule and reassigned the soul reaping to another angel."

"What was that pulse of magic?"

"Spirits don't have cell phones. That's how I communicate with the dead. I let the souls I was meant to counsel today know I won't be available."

"I wasn't on your schedule. Why did I feel it?"

"All of the dead in Purgatory felt it, but only the ones the message was intended for received it. Now, I need to go to the office and do some research. This has never happened before."

"I'm coming with you." No way in hell was he leaving her alone.

Azrael shook his head. "You're

naked."

Deirdre looked down at her spirit body, and sure enough, her ghostly gray form didn't have a speck of clothing on, which wasn't surprising. People were born naked; it made sense that they'd cross over that way too. "Then I'll get dressed."

She retrieved her shirt from the floor, but as she slipped her arms through the sleeves and put it over her head, it dropped right off her as if she didn't exist. "What in Lilith's name?"

"The spirit form remains in the clothes—or lack thereof—that the person had on when they passed. You'll be naked until we can get your soul back into your body."

She lifted her arms and dropped them at her sides. "Fuck me."

"I'll be happy to once we get this fixed." He cupped her cheek in his hand, and once again, all she felt was pressure. He needed to fix her ASAP. She missed his warmth. "I'm going to check with the other dark angels. I'm sure one of them has reanimated a vampire sometime over the millennia."

"And if they haven't?"

"We'll figure something out." He leaned over her corpse and gingerly lifted it, moving her head to the pillow before covering her with a sheet. Thankfully, he didn't completely cover her head. *Talk about feeling final.*

Azrael's cat crawled out from under the bed and jumped onto the mattress. She padded toward Deirdre's body and curled up next to her.

"Tabitha will watch over your body,

not that you have anything to worry about. No one can get into my home but me."

"Please let me come with you. I'm not shy; I don't care if people see me naked."

"Deirdre..."

"Just fly me straight there. I promise not to parade around the Underworld in my birthday suit. I'll stay in your office and be quiet." She clutched his hand. "I'm scared, Azrael. I don't want to be alone."

He gazed at her, his eyes softening as he took in her expression. With a heavy sigh, he nodded. "Don't leave my office unless I ask you to."

She held up three fingers. "Scout's honor."

"Let's go."

CHAPTER NINE

AZRAEL USHERED DEIRDRE down the hall and into his office. She might not have cared if the other angels saw her naked, but he sure did. Hell, he didn't want anyone to see her at all. It was bad enough he'd accidentally killed his girlfriend. The fact he couldn't put her back together was a crying shame. He was *the* Angel of Death, for fuck's sake. The OG. The GOAT in the reaper world.

His magic was glitching, and he needed to figure out why. Then he'd put Deirdre back together and keep his scythe locked away like he should have done from the beginning. He'd been careless, and Deirdre paid the price.

But he *would* fix her. He refused to entertain any other outcome.

"Wait here. I'll be back soon." He pulled the door halfway shut and paused. "Please don't touch anything."

"I'd promise to keep my hands in my pockets, but..." She slid her hands down her hips and shrugged. "I won't mess with your stuff."

He nodded, his grip tightening on his scythe.

"Hey..." She stopped him before he

could close the door. "I'm really sorry for touching it."

"It'll be okay. I'm going to fix this."

"I know you are." She offered him a small smile, and he closed the door before booking it down the hall to Jessie's office.

Her door stood open, and he paused to knock on the jamb. "Hey, Jess. Got a minute?"

"Sure do, Boss. How's it going with your vampire?" She grinned and closed her laptop.

Azrael's face pulled into a grimace as he shut the door and paced toward her desk.

"Uh oh." Jessie's smile faded. "What happened? Trouble in paradise?"

Azrael sank into a slate gray chair and laid his scythe across his lap. "What

I'm about to tell you doesn't leave this room."

Jessie sat in the chair opposite him. "Of course."

He ground his teeth, hesitating. Of all the dark angels, Jessie was the one he trusted most, but it didn't make the admission any easier. "Deirdre touched my scythe."

"Oh." She sat back, tilting her head. "Why would she do that? Why would you let her?"

"I didn't..." He tightened his grip on the handle. "Apparently, she has a hard time keeping her hands to herself. I warned her what it would do, but she couldn't help herself."

Jessie's gaze wandered over Severus, and she nodded appreciatively. "It is an impressive instrument. I can't blame her for being curious."

"Yeah, well, curiosity killed the vampire."

She shrugged. "What's the problem? You can put her back together."

"No, I can't. My magic is glitching."

She laughed. "Azrael, your magic doesn't glitch. I'm sure—"

"I'm not. I don't know what's happening, but she..." He clamped his mouth shut, the first inkling that he might *not* be able to fix this igniting a spark of anger in his chest. No, it wasn't anger. It was fear.

Deirdre had changed him. His capacity to care for others—for the souls he counseled—ran deeper than the steepest ravine in the Underworld, but he could always let them go. They were meant to move in and out of his life, as he was theirs. Deirdre was different. He wanted her to be forever.

His throat thickened as he looked into Jessie's eyes. "I can't lose her."

A look of surprise lifted her brows. "You're in love with her."

His grip tightened even more. "I am."

"It's about damn time." Jessie rose and strode around her desk before sitting in the chair and opening her computer. "Do you have any idea why you weren't able to reattach her soul? You followed all the steps? I mean, you created the process—you've done it for enough newbie reapers—so you must have."

"Yes." He leaned forward, lowering his voice. "Jessie, I've never done it with a vampire before."

She stopped typing to blink at him.

"Since when do you openly discuss your sex life?"

He groaned and raked a hand through his hair. "I mean I've never reanimated a vampire. The process should be the same, but it didn't work. Maybe it's not possible."

A lump formed in his throat. Perhaps Deirdre's idea that she'd cheated death before and therefore couldn't be reanimated held some merit.

No. Absolutely not. Every accidental soul severing was remediable because accidents did happen. Sometimes targets put up a fight. Other times they ran. Occasionally a scythe could strike an unintended victim, and the reanimation process could fix it. *Always.*

"See if you can find a record of someone who's done it."

"On it." Jessie's fingers flew over the keys, and Azrael racked his brain for a solution to their predicament.

Deirdre was undead, which meant, while she had technically died, her spirit never left her body. Her *body*. That had to be it. She was a borderline corpse, minus the rot. Her heart beat once every three seconds, and she had to consume the life force of others to sustain herself because she didn't have a life force of her own.

Her body was different—it wasn't alive—so the method for reattaching her spirit would be different too. Azrael mentally smacked himself upside the head. He should have known that.

"Theo has done it." Jessie's eyes darted back and forth as she read her screen. "His report says he arrived to claim the soul of a woman dying of cancer, but her vampire lover had decided to turn her that night. The vampire jumped in front of Theo's scythe, and he severed both their souls in one swipe."

Azrael's pulse sprinted. "And he successfully reanimated the vampire?"

"He did. I haven't seen him in the office this morning. Do you want to do your thing and call him here?"

He was one step ahead of her. With his eyes closed, Azrael activated his magic, opening his connection with his dark angels. Like he did with the spirits when he rescheduled their sessions, he sent out a pulse of energy. All the angels would feel it, but only Theo would receive the message.

"Ooh..." Jessie shivered and rubbed

her chest. "There'll be plenty of talk amongst the angels tonight. They'll all be wondering who got in trouble."

"And you will act as baffled as they are." Azrael rarely used this method of communication anymore. All the angels carried cell phones these days, so he reserved his magical connection for urgent matters.

"You know I will, but you might have to threaten Theo with a job reassignment to keep him quiet. He likes to run his mouth."

"I'm going to check on Deirdre in my office."

"She's here? I'd love to meet the woman who drilled her way into your heart of stone. Bring her back with you?"

Azrael stood and strode toward the door before turning to Jessie. "She's not dressed."

Her mouth dropped open. "She's naked?"

"Yes."

She laughed. "Were you banging when it happened? Oh, gods. Please tell me you were role playing. You were the Grim Reaper coming for her soul, weren't you?"

He narrowed his eyes. "We were not banging. It happened this morning as I was preparing to leave for work."

"Gotcha. It happened the morning *after* the banging. You dog."

His lips curved upward of their own volition. Being with Deirdre was so much more than banging. "I'll be right back."

He strode down the hall and entered his office to find Deirdre behind his desk, her arm outstretched, her fingers hovering over the plastic encasing the emergency ventilation activator. "Don't touch that." He crossed the room in six long strides and clutched her wrist. "I asked you not to touch anything."

"It's a big red button. How could I *not* press it? How could I not touch anything when your entire office looks like we went shopping together?"

He cast his gaze over his surroundings, and sure enough, a plethora of pink accented his black furniture. Pink throw pillows sat on the couch and in the chairs; a pink shag rug lay on the marble floor, and a painting of a pink carnation hung on the wall above his desk.

He chuckled, his heart warming at the idea that the décor she needed to see involved the two of them as a couple.

"The offices change appearance for every client. It looks this way because you want it to."

"I'm not a client."

"But you are a spirit." He tucked her ghostly hair behind her ear.

"True. What about the button? What does it do?"

He gestured to the ceiling. "That vent magically activates when a soul is ready to cross over to the spirit realm. It sucks them up, and their form passes through peacefully."

Deirdre gazed up at the vent, a look of worry tightening her eyes. "That thing could suck me up at any second, and you left me in here alone?"

"It only activates when a soul has grieved his loss of life and accepted his death. Have you done either of those things?"

She crossed her arms. "Absolutely not."

"Then there's no need to worry...unless you press that button. On rare occasions, a soul refuses to grieve and will not pass on. When that happens, I'm forced to send them over against their will. That button activates the vent manually."

Her mouth formed the shape of an O. "And it's just out here front and center, tempting people to press it? I mean, it's a giant red button. I know I'm not the only one who'd be itching to find out what it does."

He pursed his lips. "It's behind my desk and enclosed in a plastic case."

"Good point."

"If you pressed it, the vent would

shred your soul on this side and then put you back together in the spirit realm. It would be excruciatingly painful."

"Couldn't be worse than the electric shocks you gave me this morning."

"It's one hundred times worse and the only pain a spirit should feel." His phone buzzed in his pocket, and he checked the screen. A text from Jessie said *He's here.*

He looked at Deirdre in her state of undress. She splayed her fingers and then fisted her hands, her gaze bouncing around the room. Hopefully she believed him about the vent, but after the scythe incident, he'd rather not chance it.

"Come with me."

"But I'm naked."

He opened one wing and gestured for

her to come to his side. She stood next to him, and he tugged her spirit form against him, wrapping his wing around her.

"You know I love it when you hold me like this." She brushed her fingers across the underside of his wing, and he shivered.

"And you know what it does to me when you touch me like that. Please refrain while we're in the presence of the angels you're about to meet."

She pouted her lower lip. "You're no fun."

"I'm serious."

"Okay. I promise." She slipped her thumb through his back beltloop and placed her other hand in his front pocket. "Better?"

He ushered her down the hall and

slipped into Jessie's office, closing and locking the door behind them. Jessie sat perched on the edge of her desk but shot to her feet as they entered.

"You must be Deirdre. I've heard so much about you; it's nice to finally meet you."

"I'd shake your hand, but I'm not decent at the moment." Deirdre laughed. "Well, I'm never decent, but I'm not wearing clothes."

Theo sat in a leather chair and flicked his gaze between Deirdre and Azrael. "I assume the spirit you're protecting is the reason you called for me?"

Azrael nodded and moved toward him. "Tell me what you know about reanimating vampires."

Theo chuckled, rubbing his thumb and forefinger on his chin. "Wait. Are you telling me the great and powerful Az accidentally killed a vampire, and now he can't put her back together?"

"That's exactly what I'm telling you, and if word of it leaves this room, you'll be working cleanup duty in the tarpits. Understood?"

He swallowed hard. "Yep. Message received."

"Your record says you reanimated a vampire. Tell me how you did it."

Theo shrugged. "Same as anyone else. I used my scythe to put him back into his body, and his soul snapped into place. Did that not work with your vampire?" He looked at Deirdre, and Azrael instinctively tightened his wing around her.

"No, it didn't. There must be something else you did. Something different."

"If I did anything differently, I didn't realize it. I jetted as soon as I put the guy back together so I wouldn't become his next meal." He looked at Deirdre again. "No offense."

"None taken. A vampire's got to eat."

Azrael ground his teeth. The situation was beyond frustrating and heading toward dire. He had no idea how long Deirdre had before her body would reject her soul permanently. "You must not be remembering everything. Think, Theo."

Theo screwed his mouth over to the side, staring at the ceiling for an excruciatingly long moment. "I've got nothing. If that's all, I have a new soul to reap." He rose to his feet.

Azrael tensed. "I need to see what happened. Show me."

The reaper sank back onto his seat, his shoulders slumping. "Oh man. You're going to do that mindfuck thing to me, aren't you?"

"Hold up," Deirdre said. "I might be dead, but as long as I exist, the only person Azrael will be fucking is me."

Jessie flashed him a knowing smile. "Don't worry, Deirdre. He's just going to look inside Theo's mind so he can see what happened through his eyes. No actual fucking is involved."

Deirdre relaxed beside him. "Okay. Then do it, babe. Do whatever you have to do because I am not ready to be fully dead. Hell, I wasn't even ready to be undead way back when, but here I am."

Theo's nostrils flared as he let out a slow breath. "Go straight to the memory you need. No poking around for the other juicy bits."

"I'm not interested in your bits, juicy or not."

Jessie laughed. "Oh, now I've got to know what you want to hide. You're lucky I don't have his ability. I'd be juicing your bits for everything they've got."

"Ew." Deirdre scrunched her nose in a most adorable way. "Please just go for the info you need. The last thing I want to see is angel juice all over the floor."

"You better bring the memory front and center so I can find it easily," Azrael said, and he focused his energy, reaching out with his mind into Theo's. An image of the reaper Michael lying naked in the bed flashed before his eyes, and Azrael quickly diverted his attention from the memory. He definitely did not want to know about the juicy bits.

"Sorry, man." Theo shrugged. "Can't get him off my mind. Try this one."

He presented the memory, and Azrael dug in deep, experiencing it in vivid detail.

Theo entered the room and found the woman lying in bed, her hand held by a vampire at her side. Azrael felt Theo's heart ache in the memory, both for the agony the woman had endured and the pained expression on the vampire's face.

"You can't take her," the vampire said, his gaze never leaving the woman's face. "I'm going to turn her."

Theo tilted his head, sympathy knotting in his stomach. "She doesn't want to be turned."

"I don't care. I won't lose her." The

vampire choked down a sob.

"You are grieving," Theo said.

"Of course I'm grieving," he growled. "I already watched my first wife grow old and die. Everyone I've ever known has died, and I have grieved them all. I won't go through it again."

Azrael inhaled sharply, the familiarity of the vampire's situation jerking him from Theo's memory. He understood exactly how the man felt.

"What did you see?" Deirdre rested her ghostly hand against his chest, and the death chill seeped through his shirt.

He fought a shiver. "Nothing useful yet. I'm going back in."

Theo clutched his head, shuddering dramatically. "Make it fast. It feels like a feather duster running over my brain."

Azrael inhaled deeply, steeling himself for the sad scene.

"I'm sorry," Theo said to the vampire. "It's her time." He moved toward the bed and swiped his scythe at the woman, but the vampire threw himself over her dying body. Theo's blade passed through them both, severing their souls at once. "Shit," he grumbled.

The vampire's and the woman's spirits stood next to the bed, looking down at their bodies.

"Oh, Victor. What have you done?" the woman asked.

"I was trying to save you."

"I didn't want to be saved."

"Well, now I can come with you. Wherever you're going, I'll be with you."

Theo cringed. "It's not your time, man.

I wasn't supposed to reap your soul, so I have to reanimate you."

"But I..."

"He's right, my love. It's not your time to go. We both know that."

The vampire sighed, defeated. "Can I have a few more minutes with her? She hasn't been able to speak in so long."

Theo checked his watch. "Twenty minutes. Say everything you need to say. I'll be right outside, and I will know if you try to get away."

"I'll make sure he stays put," the woman said. "Thank you."

Twenty minutes later, Theo returned to the room to reanimate the vampire. Just as Azrael had taught the reapers, he had the vampire's spirit hold the scythe as he lay into the body. A pop sounded as the soul rejoined with the corpse, and *the vampire stood, peering down at the woman, tears running down his pale cheeks.*

Azrael jerked from the memory. He'd seen enough. Tightening his wing around Deirdre's spirit, he gestured to the door. "Thank you, Theo. I'll handle it from here."

Theo scratched his head and stood. As he strode to the door, Azrael stopped him with a heavy hand on his shoulder. "Nothing leaves this room."

He chuckled. "No worries, Boss. I don't want you poking around in my head again. I'll keep my mouth shut if you promise no more mindfucks."

"Deal."

As the door clicked shut, Deirdre looked up at Azrael with hope in her eyes. "You know how to fix me now?"

He pressed his lips to her cold forehead. "I..."

Her form flickered, and she gasped. "What's happening to me? Am I crossing over? I can't cross over. Turn your vent off!"

He cupped her chin in his hand. "You're not crossing over; you're running out of energy."

"What does that mean?" Panic laced her words.

"You're about to blink out and go into limbo. It's a state of suspended animation that all spirits go into after they've been interacting with the living for too long."

"I'm scared."

"It sounds frightening, but it's peaceful," Jessie reassured her. "It's like sleeping. When you come to, you'll feel as good as new."

"Where will I wake up?"

"In the same place you blink out. I'll fly you home quickly so you'll wake up there."

"You don't have any killer vents that'll whisk me away while I'm sleeping?"

"None. I promise." He walked her out of the office and flew straight to his home, her form becoming more transparent by the second. As he stepped inside and laid her on the couch, Tabitha jumped, attempting to climb into her lap, but she blinked out, fading from their plane.

He sank onto the chair, and his cat jumped into his lap instead. "I don't know what to do, Tabs. Theo didn't do anything differently when he reanimated the vampire than what I did for Deirdre. It makes no sense why her body is already rejecting her soul."

And if he couldn't figure it out fast, they were screwed.

CHAPTER TEN

DEIRDRE WOKE WITH a start, but she kept her eyes closed. It was a dream. It had to be. Everything that happened today was one long, horrible, extremely detailed nightmare, and when she opened her eyes, she would find herself in Azrael's bed with him lying by her side. She would. She had to.

Of course, if she believed the lie she was telling herself, she wouldn't have hesitated. She'd have opened her damn eyes immediately because who wouldn't want to see a naked, smokin' hot Azrael first thing?

Just get it over with, Dee. She let out a dramatic sigh and lifted her lids. Nope, she was not in Azrael's bed like she'd hoped. Instead of feeling soft satin sheets, she felt smooth leather beneath her, and nothing covered her naked body.

"Dammit. Dammit all to hell." She had... What did Azrael call it? Right, she'd *blinked out.* Swinging her legs over the side of the couch, she sat up and stretched her arms over her head. "Azrael?"

Tabitha darted into the room and

jumped onto the couch. "Meow."

"Hey there, beautiful. Where's your daddy?" She stroked her hand down the cat's back. Tabitha's fur was soft, but in her spirit form, Deirdre felt no warmth emanating from the feline.

The door swung open, and Azrael strode in, his solemn expression morphing into a sad smile as his gaze met hers. "Welcome back. How are you feeling?"

"Aside from being dead when I don't want to be, that was the best sleep I've had in my life."

"Do you mind if I come in?" Jessie hesitated in the doorway. Her brown hair was swept up in a twist, and she wore a killer black pencil skirt with a gorgeous obsidian silk blouse.

"If you don't mind a buck-naked dead

vampire sitting on the couch." She looked at Azrael. "Will you get me a blanket so I can cover up?"

He sank down beside her, and Tabitha climbed into his lap. "It would fall right through your shoulders. The dead remain in the clothes they passed in until they complete the grieving process. That's just the way it is."

Deirdre scoffed. "I've got nothing to grieve because you're going to put me back together."

Azrael flicked his gaze to Jessie as she sat in the chair, and something passed between them. Maybe it was just a look, or maybe Azrael was using his angel telepathy, but whatever it was, it didn't look good.

"You *are* going to fix me." She looked from Azrael to Jessie and then back at her angel. "Azrael?" A sickening sensation bubbled in her stomach, which was weird because she technically didn't have a stomach to bubble. What was she made of now anyway? She was solid, but she was a mist at the same time. *It doesn't matter. Focus, Dee.*

He finally looked at her. "I can't fix you until you fix yourself."

"Fix my... I'm absolutely perfect. There's nothing to fix." How dare he suggest there was something wrong with her...that *she* was the reason he couldn't figure out how to put her back together.

"Have you ever seen a counselor?" Jessie asked.

Deirdre scoffed again. Were they actually insinuating she had a mental problem? "I'm not insane."

"You don't have to be crazy to seek

therapy." Jessie folded her hands in her lap. "Even the Angel of Death needs a professional to talk to sometimes."

Jessie winked at Azrael, and a pang of jealousy twisted in Deirdre's gut...which was ridiculous. If she had a body, she'd assume the sensation was gas because she was *so* not the jealous type. In fact, her lack of jealousy was how Beau had gotten away with cheating on her for so long.

And Jessie was not her competition. Deirdre had become an excellent judge of character over the centuries, and this woman was Azrael's friend and colleague. Nothing more. *Chill the fuck out, Dee.*

She unclenched her jaw. "I saw someone once."

"So you are open to counseling."

Azrael rested his hand on her knee.

"No, I don't need it. Why do you think I do?"

"Jessie and I have been talking…"

There was that jealousy gut punch again. Immature Deirdre was screaming *why did he talk to her and not me?* in her mind, which, again, was nonsense. *Uh, maybe because you've been blinked out for the past Lilith-knows-how-long. Get a grip.*

Azrael continued, oblivious to the argument going on in Deirdre's mind. "Based on what I saw of the vampire in Theo's memory and some things you've said, we think your body is rejecting your spirit because you never grieved your first death. You never fully accepted it."

"There was nothing to grieve because

I didn't die." She lifted her hands and dropped them in her lap. "Okay, technically, I died, but only because I let that jackass Beau turn me into a vampire. I was dead for maybe two minutes tops. Why would I grieve two minutes?"

"Not the two minutes. I mean you didn't grieve the loss of your human life."

"I didn't lose my life. I'm still here. Well, I *was* still here until this morning. Or yesterday morning. How long was I out?"

"All night," Jessie said.

"You're in denial." Azrael patted her knee. "You've been in denial for two centuries."

Deirdre's mouth dropped open, and she laughed cynically. "This is unbelievable. I am so not in denial."

"Classic denial." Jessie crossed her legs and laced her fingers together on her knee.

"We might as well call her Cleopatra," Azrael said.

"Oh, that's real funny, *cher*. Ha. Ha. Ha." Mr. Broody Dark Angel had jokes now. Fang-tabulous.

"I'm sorry." He gave her thigh a squeeze. "Look, sweetheart. We have two more days before your body will reject your soul permanently. Will you humor me and talk to someone? It doesn't have to be me. You can talk to Jessie. She's the best counselor I've got."

Deirdre shrugged and crossed her arms, pouting. Was she being immature? Yes. Yes, she was. But she had accidentally killed herself, and it looked like she might be stuck this way.

They needed to cut her some slack. "It doesn't matter anyway. I'm sure my body has already started decomposing, and I do not want to walk around looking like a zombie. I might as well stay dead."

"Bodies don't decompose in the Underworld. You'll be just as gorgeous as ever if you do this for me."

She chewed her bottom lip and narrowed her eyes at him. She wanted to be reunited with her body. She missed the taste of blood and the warmth of Azrael's skin. She missed falling asleep in his arms, running her fingers through his feathers, and making him shiver with delight.

But this plan of his... "You've had twenty-four hours to think about it, and this is the best solution you've come up with? For me to see a therapist?"

"Short of me killing someone and then reanimating them just to make sure my magic isn't glitching, this is the only solution we've got."

"Well, you should do that then. We need to try everything." At least then she'd believe the problem might lie with her.

He shook his head. "That would be unethical."

"You live in the Underworld. I'm sure a lot of unethical things happen down here."

"It would be cruel to put someone through that. It's not in my nature, Deirdre. You know me better than that."

"I could try the reanimation," Jessie said.

Azrael gave her a hard look, and she raised her hands in defense. "I mean on

Deirdre. If you let me borrow your scythe, I can try putting her back together. If it works, great; if it doesn't, we'll know it's her and not your magic."

He pursed his lips thoughtfully. "That's an excellent idea."

"Yeah..." Deirdre said. "You're not the one who has to get electrocuted for the fourth time if it doesn't." Surely he wouldn't want to put her through that again.

Azrael arched a brow. "We have to try everything."

Great. He's using my own words against me. "Ugh. Fine. Let's do it." Deirdre rose and strode down the hall to the bedroom. Azrael and Jessie followed.

When she reached the doorway, she paused. She technically didn't need oxygen—because she was dead and all—

but her breath caught in her throat as she entered the room and saw herself lying there dead. *This has been the worst out-of-body experience ever.*

Azrael rubbed her back before unlocking a cabinet and retrieving his scythe. Jessie's eyes lit up as she made a grabby motion with her hands.

"I don't know why we didn't think of this sooner. Every reaper in Purgatory would die to get their hands on Severus." She snatched it from his grip the moment he offered it to her.

Deirdre laughed. "Been there; done that. Zero stars. Would not recommend."

Azrael cupped her face in his hands. "I'm glad you haven't lost your sense of humor."

"I'm a dead ringer for fun, aren't I?"

He pressed a kiss to her spirit lips,

but all she felt was a gentle pressure. Yeah, she needed to get her dead ass back into her body ASAP.

Jesse adjusted her grip on the scythe's handle and peered longingly at the blade. "It's so beautiful. It just calls to you, doesn't it?"

"Tell me about it. That's why I'm in this situation."

Azrael tucked her hair behind her ear. "Are you ready, my love?"

Her chest tightened at his words. It was a simple term of endearment, but hearing the L-word from his lips created *all* the feels inside her ghostly form. *Whoa.*

She shook herself to chase away the strange sensation. There would be time to contemplate the way he made her feel later. Maybe. If she was lucky. "Let's do this thing."

Jessie held the scythe toward her, and she gripped the blade before lying back into her body like she'd done before. The angel closed her eyes. "I am instilling you with all the reanimation magic I've got. When you're ready, let go."

Might as well. Deirdre released the blade, and for a moment, she thought it might be working. But then an electric shock strong enough to fry every light on the Eiffel Tower ricocheted through her body, sending her spirit to the ceiling with a splat.

"Ugh."

***

Azrael cringed as Deirdre hit, and when her spirit flopped down to the floor, he ran to her, kneeling by her side. "Are you okay, sweetheart?"

"I'm still dead as a door knocker, and I feel like I've been fried in a vat of oil with a dozen Boudin balls. No, I'm not okay."

"Sorry. I tried my best. I'll put this away now." Jessie returned the scythe to the closet and closed the door.

Azrael's heart ached for Deirdre. He could only imagine how painful that must have been for her, but perhaps it was what she needed to convince her she was the problem. Hopefully that was all it would take because he was out of ideas. "What would you like to try next?"

Deirdre sat up, and as her body shuddered, he instinctively wrapped his wings around her. She sighed and leaned into him, the tension in her muscles easing. "How do you always know exactly what I need?"

"I pay attention." She'd made it clear from the first time they were together that she liked being wrapped in his wings.

"That you do." She pulled from his embrace, giving him a kiss on the cheek before standing. "I don't think it's going to help, but I'll talk to Jessie."

"Oh, okay." He sounded way more disappointed than he intended, but disappointed he was. He rose to his feet and tried not to look too dejected.

"No offense, *cher*. I just think a neutral party would be best." She turned to Jessie. "When do we start?"

Jesse looked at Azrael and nodded. "I already cleared my schedule. I am all yours."

"Y'all knew I would agree to this?" She arched a brow at Azrael.

He lifted his hands. "We hoped you would." Though he'd hoped she'd want to talk to him about her past.

"You know me too well." Deirdre glanced at her body and curled her lip. "Can we do this in your office? I think I need some fresh air."

Azrael flew Deirdre to the counseling center, and as she followed Jessie to her office, he slipped into his own. The décor hadn't changed since it morphed into the aesthetic Deirdre needed, and the idea that his needs matched hers warmed his soul. They were meant to be together. Of that, he was certain. He felt it in his bones.

He hoped to Hades Jessie could guide her through her grief quickly because they were running out of time. Hell, if she could just rip off the duct tape Deirdre had wrapped around her heart, he could handle it from there. She might be their toughest case yet, but it was possible to move a soul into acceptance in the span of a few hours. He'd done it before. Jessie had too.

Some souls were more open to the idea of death. Deirdre wasn't one of them, but between Jessie and him, they could help her. They had no other choice.

He sank into his chair and drummed his fingers on his desk, trying his damnedest to squelch the worry churning in his gut. This plan *would* work. Death and transition were all about acceptance. Deirdre had died when she became a vampire, and she never grieved her loss of life, never fully accepted her transition. It made perfect sense why her body wouldn't accept her soul as it was. Her body was undead, but her spirit never got over dying.

He picked up the small pink coffin from his desk and fidgeted with the lid. He never rushed his clients, giving them all the time they needed to come to terms with their conditions. But now, for the first time in his existence, he was out of patience with the dead.

CHAPTER ELEVEN

THE MOMENT DEIRDRE stepped into Jessie's office, the aesthetic morphed into the same pink and black palette as Azrael's. Jessie gestured to a black upholstered chaise, and Deirdre sank onto it as the angel settled into a pink accent chair.

"Sorry for changing your color

scheme." Deirdre ran her hand over the fabric, circling her finger around a button on the seat.

"Don't be. It's meant to comfort you, and it gives me some insight into your needs." She sat with her knees together, facing Deirdre, her hands folded in her lap.

"Oh? What does it tell you about me?"

Jessie glanced around the room. "That you're outgoing, fun-loving, and that a little bit of Azrael has seeped into your soul."

"Psh. That man..." At the thought of her dark angel, the pink shag rug turned black. Azrael had affected her more than a little bit. "Hold on." She squinted at the accent chair, willing it to turn black, and it obeyed.

Jessie raised her brow. "Impressive."

"Huh. If I can do that, I wonder…" She closed her eyes and imagined her favorite pink catsuit hugging her body. When she lifted her lids, she was wearing it. "That's better."

Jessie blinked. "That's something I've never seen."

Deirdre ran her hands over the soft fabric. "Of course you haven't. I had it custom made."

"No, I mean I've never seen a spirit change their clothes until it was time to cross over."

Her fingers curled into fists, a cold flush of panic spreading through her chest as she peered at the vent in the ceiling. "It's not my time."

"No, it's not. Your clothes would turn pure white if it were." Jessie flashed a sympathetic smile and crossed her legs.

"Tell me about your first death."

Deirdre cringed. That was a subject she hadn't thought about in ages. In fact, she hadn't allowed herself to recall the ordeal in so long, she wasn't sure she could talk about it without breaking down. *Duh, Dee. That's kinda the point.* But still...

"Can we start with an easier topic?"

"Okay. Tell me about your relationship with Azrael."

She blew out a breath. "That one's not much easier."

"Why not?"

"It's complicated." She toyed with the button on the seat.

"Break it down for me."

She drew her shoulders toward her ears. "He's amazing. He listens to me and makes me feel seen. I feel safe with him, and he always knows exactly what I need, sometimes even before I do. The man is too good to be true, and it scares me to death." She laughed. "Literally."

"Why is that scary?"

"Because I've let myself grow fond of him. I've broken rule number one, which is *don't get attached*." She rubbed her hands over her arms absently. "I know what it'll feel like when he gets tired of me, and it won't feel good."

"Why do you think he'll get tired of you?"

"Why wouldn't he?" And that was the million-dollar question, wasn't it? She'd lost everyone else in her life. Azrael was immortal, so she wouldn't lose him to death. He'd get sick of her eventually, and that would hurt even worse.

Jessie smiled knowingly. "He hasn't

told you..."

"Told me what?"

"He's grown fond of you too. I understand your fear of losing him, but Azrael is here to stay. Have you talked to him about your insecurities?"

She scoffed. "Sweet Lilith, no. I'm a confident, kick-ass vampire. He doesn't need to know I die inside at the thought of losing him. Hell, I don't even allow myself to *think* about it. I can't tell him that."

"He's afraid of losing you too. He cares for you deeply."

"How do you know?"

"I've known Azrael my entire existence, and I have never seen him happier than he's been the past month."

"Not even when..." *He was with Nora?*

"Never. He's crazy about you, but if

you don't open up, you'll soon lose each other. Spirits can't stay in Purgatory forever."

Deirdre let out a long, slow breath. "Why not? I can still feel him. Sure, I'll miss his warmth, but we can be together if I'm a ghost. I'll adjust." And staying dead for the rest of eternity would be easier than digging up the bones of her past.

Jessie peered at the ceiling. "Eventually, you'll be forced through the vent. I understand it's rather unpleasant."

She shuddered.

"Going back to your first death. Tell me what happened."

Deirdre chewed the inside of her cheek. How bad would it be if Azrael knew the real her? He had opened up and told her about losing his first love. She didn't think any less of him for showing vulnerability. Why would he think less of her? And even if he did...even if he decided he didn't want to be with her, so what? Apparently if she didn't tell *someone* about her past, she'd be sucked into the ghost chipper and sent to the spirit realm anyway. She might not be damned if she did talk to him, but she'd certainly be damned if she didn't.

It was time to start digging. "I think I should speak to Azrael about this. He deserves to know."

Jessie smiled. "I agree."

The moment Deirdre stepped into the hallway, Jessie's office décor changed to a palette of white and soft blues. Peaceful. Serene. A feeling Deirdre hadn't experienced in centuries. Well...except when she was wrapped in Azrael's wings.

She spun in the direction of his office, and her vision swam. "Whoa." She clutched her head and shook herself to chase away the dizzying sensation before pacing down the hall. His room lay only ten yards away, but the trek felt like she'd hiked up and down every street in the French Quarter sixteen times in the middle of August. By the time she reached his open door, her form began to flicker.

No. This can't happen now.

"Azrael?" She paused in the threshold, willing herself to stay solid. "I think I'd rather talk to you, if you don't mind."

"Deirdre. Of course I don't mind." He

shot to his feet and strode toward her, stopping as his gaze took in her form. "You have clothes..."

"Not bad for a two-days-dead ghost, eh?"

"You never cease to amaze me. Come in. Let's talk."

Azrael reached for her hand, but before he could take it, her form vibrated, and she blinked out.

***

"Damn it to Hades." Azrael ground his teeth as he marched to Jessie's office. Her eyes widened as he stormed into the room, and the entire space plunged into obsidian.

"What happened?" She closed her computer, a look of alarm contorting her features.

"She blinked out."

"Already? She just came back a few hours ago."

"What did you do to her? Why did you wear her out?" He stood in front of her desk, his fists clenched.

Jessie rose to her feet. "Slow your roll, Boss. All I did was talk to her." She crossed her arms. "Do you realize how menacing you look when you act like this? It's no wonder people are afraid of you."

He took a deep breath, relaxing his posture. "I apologize."

She grinned. "It's okay. I know you wouldn't hurt a flea."

"Please tell me what happened. We don't have time for her to blink out again."

"I warmed her up for you. We chatted

for a while, and when she was finally ready to talk about her first death, she wanted to talk about it with you. That's all."

He groaned. "It was the clothes. She used all her energy forming her clothes."

"That must be it. She figured out how to draw on the magic of the building, but magic always comes at a price."

"Fuck." He raked his hands through his hair. "She blinked out in my office. That's where I'll be until she comes back."

She lifted a finger to stop him. "Might I offer a suggestion?"

"Go ahead."

"Find something to keep yourself busy. Maybe call in a client or two for a session they missed. I know you, and you're going to stew until you drive yourself crazy if you don't."

"I'm not going to stew," he said through clenched teeth.

Jessie shook her head. "Famous last words."

Azrael returned to his office, and, as usual, Jessie was right. He did stew. He sat at his desk and stared at the clock, watching the minutes tick by until he was nothing but a big, brooding ball of worry.

"I can't sit here like this." He needed *something* to pass the time, so he might as well go with his therapist's advice. She'd never steered him wrong before. Closing his eyes, he sent out a pulse, calling Joey Sinclair into his office.

"I thought I'd gotten time off for good behavior." The spirit sauntered into the room and plopped onto the couch as the scenery morphed into a drab financial office.

"I have some free time after all." Azrael moved to the chair across from him. "Tell me how you're feeling."

He listened to Joey drone on and on about how he'd been cheated out of his time on Earth. The ghost was firmly in the anger stage now, which was good. Only two more steps to go. Just as he was about to launch into a monologue about all the so-called *good* things he'd done with his life, a vibration formed in the air behind Azrael.

Deirdre blinked back in. "Oh damn. I'm naked again. Let me make some clothes."

"No!" Azrael leaped over the back of his chair and wrapped his wings around her. "That's why you blinked out. Don't do it again."

She stroked the underside of his wing. "Is it really, or do you just want to keep me naked?"

He cleared his throat and jerked his head toward Joey, who sat grinning like a fool on the sofa.

"Oh, hello." Deirdre waved.

Joey chuckled. "Is this my reward for living a good life? Maybe I am ready to die then."

Azrael glared at the spirit. "We'll finish our session tomorrow. Leave now."

"C'mon. At least let me watch."

"Get out." Azrael sent out a pulse of magic, and the ghost flew backward through the wall.

"Whoa. I thought we were solid here in the Underworld," Deirdre said.

"It only seems that way to help spirits

with the transition. You can pass through walls if you believe you can...or if I make you."

"Like how I could make clothes?"

"Yes, but that drained you. I need you present, so you'll have to stay naked for now."

"Hmm..." She turned and slid her arms around his waist. "Then I think you should be naked too. It's only fair."

He folded his wings against his back and unwrapped himself from her tempting embrace. "As soon as we get you reanimated, we can be naked together for as long as you like."

"Forever?" She bit her bottom lip, her brow scrunching as if she hadn't meant to say it.

But he was so glad she did.

"There is nothing I want more than to

spend forever with you."

Her lip slipped from the clutches of her teeth as she smiled. "Then let's talk so maybe we can make that happen."

They sat side by side on the couch, and Deirdre folded one leg beneath her, angling to face him. "Jessie kept asking me to tell her about my first death, so I guess I'll start there."

Azrael nodded, silently urging her to continue.

She sighed. "I told you about my sire, Beau, and how he left me five years after he turned me."

"Yes."

She nodded, her gaze growing distant. "I never wanted to be a vampire. I was stupid to let him turn me, but I was young and dumb, and so in love with the idea of love, I couldn't see him for what he truly was."

"What do you mean?"

"I came from a wealthy family. I was well-educated, had a bright future ahead of me. I lived with my parents and three sisters, and I was happy. Life was good. Then I met Beau. I didn't know what he was at first, of course, but he wooed me. He did everything right; he was the perfect gentleman. My family adored him. I found it odd that he only came to see me at night, but he insisted his job didn't allow him time during the day."

She inhaled deeply, drawing her shoulders toward her ears. "Eventually, I got suspicious and thought he had another woman. That's when he told me he was a vampire. He made it sound so glamorous; I let him feed on me. Of course, now I realize he was feeding on me all along and using his magic to make me forget, but whatever. It's what vamps do." She shrugged.

"He told me he loved me. He said he wanted to spend forever with me...and he wanted me to stay young forever. And, well, there was only one way that could happen, right?" She scoffed, shaking her head.

"So I did it. I let him turn me. He took me away from my family, my friends. He took everything from me, and I let him because I was 'in love.'" She made air quotes.

"In the beginning, he kept me busy, taking me to balls, going hunting every night. I never had time to miss my family. Then, one night, I woke up, and he was gone. Just gone. He didn't say goodbye, didn't leave a note... Nothing."

She rubbed one arm.

Azrael's heart ached for her. "That must have been painful."

"It was, but I'm over it." She waved away his statement like she didn't have a care in the world, but he knew she did. She was hurting. Had been for centuries.

"Are you?"

"I have to be. The five years we were together, he taught me how to ignore the pain. I gave myself a good fifteen minutes to be sad, a night and a half to be angry as all get-out, and then I went back to being busy. It wasn't until I met the woman he'd dumped before me that I realized what he really was."

She stared blankly ahead until Azrael rested his hand on her knee.

"Her name was Abigail. She was also twenty-two when he turned her, but she only got three years out of him before he left her high and dry. She told me about Elizabeth, the woman who came before her." She leaned her head back and inhaled deeply. She was finally allowing the pain inside.

Azrael took her hand. "He had a pattern."

"Beau was a serial killer. Only, he didn't leave his victims dead; he turned us into vampires and then left us alone." She swallowed hard. "He took everything from me, and then he discarded me. My family and friends thought I was dead, so I watched from a distance as they grew old and died. Everyone I ever loved was gone. I was alone, and I've been alone ever since."

She looked into his eyes. "The woman you think you know is a lie, Azrael. It's a mask. I'm a thrill seeker, a good-time girl, the life of the party—only because when I stop, all I'm left with is emptiness. I'm nothing." A tear slid down her cheek, and he held her hand between both of his.

Instinct told him to comfort her. If he wrapped her in his wings, he could ease her pain, but she needed to feel it. She had to grieve.

"I never got to say goodbye." She straightened her spine. "Fuck Beau. I swear to Lilith if I ever see him again, I'll tear him into so many pieces, no one will know he even existed."

Tears streamed from her eyes, and she wiped them away with her fingertips. "What the hell is this? Ghosts shouldn't have bodily fluids."

Azrael chuckled. "Tears help you

through the grieving process."

She looked at her hands. "I never grieved."

"No, you didn't."

She sobbed and leaned against him, unleashing centuries of suppressed sadness. He held her against his chest, longing to take the pain from her. "Let it all out, sweetheart."

He lost track of how long he sat there holding her, her shoulders lifting and lowering with her sobs, but her tears finally subsided, and she sat up, wiping beneath her eyes.

"Damn, that felt good. I haven't cried since before I died. I just..." She laughed, unbelieving. "If I would have known how much better I'd feel if I let myself experience the pain, I would have done it a long time ago. I guess Beau damaged me in more ways than one."

"I will help you heal."

She smiled softly and stroked his cheek. "How much time do we have left?"

He glanced at the clock. "Twelve hours."

"I think I'm ready." She rose to her feet. "Should we go home and try again?"

"Are you sure? You've accepted that you died and were given a new, but very different, life?"

"I have. I mean, it wasn't the life I had planned for myself, but I made do. My second life has been fang-tastic, if I say so myself. Then I met you, and I got to experience what it really feels like to fall in love, and... Even if it doesn't work, and I have to go to the spirit world, that's okay. It was worth it to be able to tell you I love you."

His breath caught, the words he wanted to say getting stuck in his throat.

"Let's go." She jerked her thumb toward the door, and a long white dress appeared on her body. Her eyes widened, and she looked down before lifting her gaze to his eyes. "Uh oh."

The ceiling vent kicked on, and Azrael's blood turned to ice. "No!"

Deirdre's form shimmered, and as it began lifting from the floor, Azrael threw his wings around her.

But he was too late. She was gone.

CHAPTER TWELVE

DEIRDRE STOOD IN the center of a gleaming white room, surrounded by dozens of spirits milling about, all wearing the same white gown she now wore. The floor looked like a cloud, with mist billowing around her feet, and she couldn't tell if the ceiling was painted to look like a clear blue sky or if there wasn't a ceiling at all.

The last thing she remembered before she ended up here was Azrael's wings encircling her. Then she got sucked up into that devil-damned vent.

She spun in a circle, frantically searching the walls and kicking the mist away so she could see the floor. If she left Purgatory through a vent, the entrance to this place had to be the other end of the same duct. She ran toward the wall in front of her, but as she moved, it seemed to drift farther away. *Fang-fucking-tastic.*

"Oh, come on. This can't be all there is to the afterlife." She made a sharp right and headed toward an angel standing next to some sort of kiosk.

The woman had curly red hair, porcelain skin, and white wings. She wore white slacks and an apron, which reminded Deirdre of Flo from the insurance commercials. Her nametag read Jeannie. "Hi there!" She beamed a smile. "Welcome to the spirit realm. Please pick your paradise." Jeannie tapped the kiosk screen, and an array of images appeared.

"There's been a mistake. I'm not supposed to be here."

"This is temporary. Consider it the Grand Central Station of the spirit realm. Once you pick your paradise, you'll be exactly where you're supposed to be."

Deirdre shook her head frantically. "I'm supposed to be in Purgatory."

Jeannie pursed her lips. "That's a new one. I suppose we can whip up a paradise to resemble it, if that's what you want."

"Purgatory *is* my paradise. You have to send me back."

She laughed. "Don't be silly. Souls can't stay in Purgatory."

"I know, but my body is there too. I'm telling you this is all a mistake. I'm not supposed to be in the spirit realm."

Jeannie scowled. "Your reaper failed to prepare you properly. What's their name so I can report them?"

"It's Azrael. Yes! Call him!"

"Azrael? He doesn't make mistakes. Something must be wrong."

She held in her groan and forced a smile. How could an angel be so dense? Weren't they supposed to be perfect?

"That's what I've been trying to tell you. Me being here is a mistake, so if you'll show me the vent that leads back to Purgatory, I'll be on my way."

"Oh dear." Jeannie tapped the kiosk, and the screen went blank. "I'm afraid there's no way out of the spirit realm."

"What do you mean there's no way out? There has to be a way out. I'm. Not. Supposed. To. Be. Here." She wanted to shake the woman, but she fisted her hands at her sides instead.

"There is no way out for spirits. It's forbidden." Jeannie clicked her tongue and shook her head. "No, you're definitely not ready for paradise."

"Ugh. Look, I've only got twelve hours to..."

"Robert," Jeannie spoke into her wristwatch, "I need a transfer to the DMS."

Another white-winged angel appeared beside her. "Who screwed up this time?"

"Azrael, believe it or not."

"No kidding?" Robert laughed. "I suppose there's a first time for everything."

"No! Azrael didn't screw up. I did. Just...please take me back to Purgatory." Why wouldn't these angels listen to her?

"Come with me." Robert clutched her arm, and, in a blink, Deirdre found herself standing in a drab beige office. Aluminum folding chairs lined one wall, and a woman with frizzy gray hair sat knitting behind the counter a few yards away.

"Where are we?" She turned to Robert, but he'd disappeared, leaving her alone in a waiting room that reminded her so much of boring places like the DMV, she wanted to puke.

"Perfect," she scoffed. One minute she was given the option of what she wanted heaven to look like, and now she stood smack in the middle of Hell.

She smoothed her white gown over her hips and strode to the counter, but the woman didn't look up from her knitting. Deirdre cleared her throat. When the woman still didn't acknowledge her, she drummed her nails on the counter and glanced at the wall behind her. A white sign that had yellowed with age read, "Welcome to the DMS," and beneath that, it said, "Department of Misplaced Souls."

Misplaced? Yes! That was exactly what she was: a misplaced soul. She should have been placed back inside her body, but instead she stood in the most utterly mind-numbing place she'd ever encountered, trying to get the attention of a woman who was oblivious to her presence.

"Excuse me, ma'am. I need some help getting back to Purgatory."

The woman continued ignoring her.

"Ma'am?" Deirdre flattened her palms on the counter, her index finger tapping as she ground her teeth. Was she invisible? *Sweet Lilith, what if I am?* Then what would she do?

She lifted her gaze, and, next to the DMS sign, hung a square electronic device. "Now Serving" was written in white above a glowing red number eighty-seven.

"That wasn't there before. Apparently I have to take a number?" She looked at the woman but got no response, so she turned around and padded into the waiting area. Honestly, she was the only misplaced soul in the room; why in Hades would she need to take a number?

She found the red plastic container that spit out the numbers, and she yanked one out. "Six-hundred and fifty-three? You've got to be kidding me." Her twelve hours would run out long before Grandma Betsy over there called for her. She'd already lost enough time trying to explain her situation to the angels. Hell, maybe she'd lost it all. Who knew how time worked in the spirit realm?

As she thought about time, a comical clock shaped like a black cat appeared on the wall. The clock face, centered in the cat's stomach area, read ten o'clock, but Deirdre had no idea what time it was when the stupid vent sucked her up here. The cat had large white eyes that moved from side to side in time with its tail wagging the seconds away.

Deirdre stepped toward it and clutched the tail. Half of her hoped stopping this clock would actually stop time in the spirit realm. Downright ridiculous, she knew, but it was worth a shot. The other half of her wanted to rip the damn thing off the wall for mocking her.

"Don't touch that." Grandma Betsy finally acknowledged her presence.

Deirdre released the taunting tail, and the clock disappeared. "Sorry. Bad habit." She strode toward the desk. "I need help."

"You'll have to wait until your number is called, dear." She set her knitting aside and rolled her chair toward a computer that looked like it came from 1998. It had a bulky CRT monitor that took up half the desk, and as she wiggled the mouse, the machine whirred to life.

"I don't have time to wait."

"You're dead. You have all the time in the world."

An old-fashioned alarm clock appeared on the counter next to her, and Deirdre fisted her hands, focusing on the sensation of her nails digging into her palms. She was just about ready to scream when the alarm sounded, the tiny hammer swinging back and forth, whacking the bells on top of the clock and sounding like a jackhammer in her skull.

Though she wanted to slam her hand down on the vexing thing, she let it ring.

Hopefully it would bug Granny as much as it did her and move things along.

The woman smiled sweetly and punched a few keys. "Number 653?" The clock disappeared, and the glowing red number on the wall flipped to Deirdre's.

"Yes, that's me." She shoved her paper number toward Granny, who took it, peered at it for fucking ever, and then dropped it in a bin next to her clunky computer.

"Welcome to the DMS. Name, please?"

"Deirdre Boudreaux. There's been a mistake. I'm not supposed to be here."

Granny nodded, punching the keys with her index fingers. "No one is, dear. We'll get you where you're going soon, though I'm not sure why you're in a rush."

Deirdre groaned. "Please. I'm running

out of time."

A cuckoo clock appeared on the wall, and a skeleton bird screeched as it struck eleven. "How has an hour already passed?"

"Time flies on your way to Hell. The more impatient you are, the faster it goes."

"Ugh. Wait." She snapped her head toward the woman. "On my way to where?"

"To Hell, of course." She looked at Deirdre like she was crazy and heaved herself up from the chair. "Come on back, and we'll get your orientation started."

Deirdre's mouth dropped open, a thousand thoughts ricocheting through her brain, but she couldn't grab on to one. What in Lilith's name was going on?

AZRAEL

The woman opened a door, motioning for her to follow, and Deirdre shuffled through it as if on autopilot.

Granny took her to a room that looked like it belonged in a 1990s high school, complete with plastic chairs with attached desks and a television on a cart with a VCR on the shelf beneath. "Have a seat." She motioned to a desk before inserting a tape into the VCR.

"There's been a mistake." Deirdre was beginning to sound like a broken record.

"Indeed there has, dear, but we're going to remedy it." She pressed play on the VCR and sat behind a metal teacher's desk as the video began.

A demon with red skin and black eyes appeared on the screen. "Greetings. We apologize for the confusion you must be experiencing. Your dark angel believed you belonged in paradise, but they were wrong. This video will serve as your orientation to Hell."

"No. No!" Deirdre slammed her hand on the desk and shot to her feet. "My angel didn't make a mistake. I touched his scythe, and he was going to put me back together. Why won't anyone listen to me?"

Granny clicked her tongue. "You have to watch the video, dear."

"Let me call Azrael. He'll sort this out."

"This is processing for Hell, not jail. You don't get to make a phone call." She opened a drawer and pulled out another knitting set. Was that a beanie with holes for horns?

Deirdre clutched her hands over her chest. "You call him, then. I saw a phone on your desk out there. Just call him up, and he'll tell you I don't belong in Hell. I need to go back to Purgatory."

"I'm afraid that's not possible. Dark angels aren't allowed contact with those of us in the spirit realm, and there's no way back to Purgatory. The ventilation system only works one way."

"Please." Deirdre choked on a sob. This couldn't be happening. She *finally* let go of the past and found someone she wanted to spend forever with, and now she was on her way to being tortured for all eternity. *So unfair.* "Can't you do anything?"

Granny sighed, her brow lifting in sympathy. "If you don't belong in paradise, there's only one place you can go."

"I never meant for this to happen."

She plopped into the chair, letting her elbows thunk on the desk and holding her head in her hands.

"The road to Hell is paved—"

"With one wicked ventilation system."

CHAPTER THIRTEEN

"FUCK. FUCK, FUCK, *fuck*!" Azrael dashed down the hall and threw open the door to Jessie's office. Bright yellows and oranges in psychedelic swirls nearly blinded him, but the panic coursing through his veins forced him forward despite the client sitting on her couch. "She's gone. Deirdre is gone."

"Let's continue our session tomorrow," Jessie said to the spirit.

The ghost took one look at Azrael fuming and shot through the door. Jessie stood and strode around her desk toward him. "What do you mean she's gone? Where did she go?"

"Through the fucking vent." Azrael fisted his hands, and her entire office turned to black stone. This could not be happening. "I have to get her back. I have to get into the spirit realm."

"Okay, slow down. Was it..." She cringed. "A forced extraction?"

"No. She accepted it. She poured her heart out to me, and she accepted everything she'd been through. She finally found peace, and then the devil-damned vent sucked her up, and she was gone."

His heart wrenched at the thought of her up there all alone. "She must be so scared right now. She wasn't prepared for that. She won't know what to do once she's there."

"Do you think she would pick a paradise?"

"No. No, she wouldn't do that. She'd want to come back. I know she would." Because if she did pick a paradise, she was really *gone*. He'd have lost her forever.

He refused to accept that.

Jessie paced in front of her desk. "I don't understand how she got sucked up in the first place. Surely she didn't accept dying by touching your scythe?"

"Of course not. She..." His stomach dropped, the edges of his vision blurring as he sank onto the arm of the chair.

"What did she say, Azrael?" Jessie placed a hand on his shoulder.

"She said if our plan didn't work, and she had to go to the spirit realm, it was worth it to have the chance to tell me she loves me." His throat thickened, and he looked at his friend. "I didn't tell her I love her too."

"Oh, wow. She really is gone."

"I have to get her back." He rose and paced the length of the office. "She's probably lost somewhere, trying to find her way home. I'm going up there."

"They won't let you in. You know dark angels aren't allowed past the gate."

His jaw ticked. "I can be very persuasive."

Jessie crossed her arms. "Not with a light angel. They won't put up with your level of grumpiness."

"I can be nice."

She cocked her head. "You'll have to smile."

He could do that. Hell, he'd smiled more in the past month than he had in his entire existence. "No problem."

"Lucifer will be livid."

His nostrils flared as he blew out a breath. "Do you not want me to get her back?"

She raised her hands. "I do, but I want you to think this through. Is barging into the spirit realm with your fists clenched and your feathers ruffled really the best way to do this? Take some time to formulate a plan."

"I don't have time to sit and think. This is the only way. If anyone asks, tell them I went topside to see Deirdre."

Jessie's expression softened into one

of sympathy. "I'll cover for you. Good luck."

"Thanks, Jess." He was going to need it.

Azrael left the office and soared through Purgatory, the scenery blurring as his mind reeled. How could he have let this happen? He hadn't even stopped to consider what might ensue if Deirdre moved into acceptance while in his office. That fucking vent acted automatically; the red button on the wall only allowed him to turn it on, not off. Even the Grim Reaper himself didn't have the power to stop the spirit realm from summoning a soul.

As he reached the northernmost wall, he flapped his wings harder, making the vertical ascent through a crystal-lined tunnel that sparkled like stars in the night sky used to before humans dimmed the glow with their electric lights. The passage narrowed, and he drew his wings inward, moving them in a smaller, quicker motion to complete his climb.

As he reached the top, he burst through a billowing cloud and drifted to the floor. Mist swirled around his feet, parting as his dark magic opposed the light. He turned in a circle to take in the scene, but there was nothing to see. White mist stretched into eternity in every direction.

He trudged forward through the fog. Magic up here worked differently than down below, and if he could get his head straight and focus, he'd find the gate. Intention was everything in the spirit realm.

Pausing, he took a deep breath, calming his racing heart as best he could and imagining himself finding the entrance. He continued his trek, and a white plaster wall with a blue door appeared a few yards ahead. Not exactly the golden gates he'd expected, but whatever. As long as the door could get him inside to Deirdre, he'd take it.

He pounded his fist against the wood and stepped back to wait. He counted to ten, and when no one answered, he knocked again. "I don't have time for this."

Five seconds later, he lifted his arm to knock a third time, and the door swung open. A light angel with golden-blond hair and pristine white wings opened his mouth to speak, but his eyes widened as recognition dawned on his face.

"Azrael?" He stepped through the door, closing it behind him. "What are you doing up here?"

"I need inside. I have to retrieve a soul."

The man clasped his hands in front of him and widened his stance. "You know that's not possible. Dark angels are forbidden from entering the spirit realm."

He stepped toward him, but the angel didn't waver. "You need to make an exception. This is an emergency."

"I didn't make the rule, so I can't make the exception."

Azrael huffed, his hands curling into fists as he glowered at the angel. "Move away from the door."

He laughed. "Light angels aren't afraid of Death. You have no power here."

He unclenched his fists and loosened his jaw, remembering Jessie's advice. *Be nice.* He forced a smile. "What's your name, friend?"

"It's Robert."

Azrael nodded. "Robert, I made a mistake. A soul went through the vent a while ago, and she wasn't meant to leave Purgatory."

"All souls are meant to leave Purgatory."

"Not this one," he snapped, which was not the way to deal with this guy. "My apologies. Deirdre, the lost soul, is my girlfriend. She was separated from her body in an accident, and I was going to reanimate her. It was not her time to pass."

Robert's brow rose. "The blonde

woman? I remember her. I took her to the DMS for processing."

"Great. Where is the DMS? I'll go get her and take her home."

"I'm afraid that won't be possible. The Department of Misplaced Souls is inside the spirit realm, and…"

"Dark angels are forbidden from entering." Azrael ground his teeth. "What's she being processed for?"

"For her entry into Hell. She didn't belong in paradise, so that's the only other place we could send her."

"You're sending her to Hell?" This couldn't be. If Deirdre spent eternity being tortured by demons, he couldn't live with himself. He would not let that happen.

"She's probably already there. It's hard to say because time is merely a construct. It works differently here."

"Shit." He turned on his heel and marched toward the exit.

"It was nice meeting you," Robert called. "You're a legend up here, you know."

He'd be a legendary fuck up if he didn't snatch her out of whatever torment they had planned for her. Demons, he could handle. These light angels and their rule-following could suck it.

Azrael tucked his wings against his back and dove into the tunnel, free falling all the way back to Purgatory. As the passage widened at the end, he opened his wings, catching the wind and drifting to the ground. The moment his feet hit the stone, he headed straight home to pick up his scythe and made a beeline for the gates of Hell.

A beefy demon named Beetle with brick-red skin and black eyes sat at a desk made from bone. He didn't look up from his computer as Azrael approached, so he cleared his throat and hit his scythe on the floor to get his attention.

Beetle sighed and flicked his gaze to Azrael before returning to the computer screen. Resting his finger on the trackpad, he scrolled, laughing at something he'd seen. No doubt it was something ridiculous like a human getting hit in the balls. These lower-level demons had moronic senses of humor.

"Beetle," Azrael said in his most commanding tone.

The demon reluctantly tore his gaze away from his screen and glowered. "What?"

"I'm here to retrieve a soul. Bring me Deirdre Boudreaux."

He scoffed. "Are you here on Lucifer's orders? I never got no notice."

"This is *my* order."

Beetle chuckled and rubbed the spittle from his chin. "If it ain't from Lucifer, I ain't doing it."

Sweet Cerberus, Azrael hated demons. He gritted his teeth. "Yes, you are."

Beetle crossed his thick arms, flexing his biceps, trying—and failing—to look menacing. "Who's gonna make me?"

Azrael clicked his tongue and gave his scythe a sideways glance as he spun it around in his hand. One swipe of the blade and this insolent demon would find out what it was like to be on the other side of Hell's gates.

Beetle sniffed and pursed his lips, the silent threat received loud and clear. "What's the name again?"

"Deirdre Boudreaux." Azrael tugged his phone from his pocket while Beetle searched for her name. "Holy fuck. Make it fast."

He'd lost six hours on his trip to the spirit realm. Robert wasn't kidding when he said time worked differently there. Every muscle in his body tensed, and he ground his teeth so hard, sharp pain shot through his jaw. "What's taking so long?"

"There's millions of names to search through. Have a little patience, reaper."

Azrael took a deep breath, counting backward from ten like Jessie had taught him to do. When he reached zero, he started over again, his hand tightening on the handle of his scythe.

"Found her." Beetle squinted at the screen. "She ain't here yet."

"Where is she?"

"She's still in orientation at the DMS."

Azrael grunted. There was no way in Lucifer's realm that light angel would let him pass. He'd have to wait until Deirdre arrived in Hell. "What torture is planned for her when she gets here?"

Beetle let out a long whistle. "A replica of you will skin her alive every day for the rest of eternity."

Oh, hell no. He could not let that happen. The skinning would be bad enough on its own, but the betrayal she would feel thinking Azrael was doing it would crumble her.

He flew back up the tunnel as fast as his wings would take him. His intent was so focused, the door stood two feet away from the exit when he arrived. He took a deep breath, steeling himself for what he was about to do. Opening up to Deirdre had been easy because she was his soulmate. He could talk to Jessie because she was his only friend, and he'd been her mentor since the beginning of her existence. Spilling his guts to this light angel and begging him for help was another story.

He knocked lightly on the door and straightened his spine. This time, he counted backward from fifty, and when he reached the number three, Robert opened the door.

The light angel took one look at Azrael's scythe and stepped back. "Are you trying to threaten me?"

"What?" He looked at his blade. "No, I

was threatening a demon. I just want to talk to you." He took a step toward him. "She's still at the DMS. I need to get her before she's sent to Hell."

"You know that's not possible."

"Please, I'm begging you. Hear me out." He pleaded with his eyes and did his best to relax his normally brooding posture.

Robert peered into the spirit realm and nodded once before stepping through the door and closing it. A table appeared beside them, white with two chairs on either side, and he gestured to it. "Have a seat."

Though he was tempted to barge through the door and leave Robert out in the ether, Azrael sank into a chair and rested Severus against the table. "This entire ordeal is my fault. She came here because I screwed up, and she needs to come home. Deirdre is the most amazing woman I have ever met. She has changed me. The only reason I can sit here and tell you this is because she taught me how to love again."

He laid his hands flat on the table. "She accidentally touched the blade of my scythe, and it severed her soul. I tried to reanimate her, but I couldn't, because she never accepted her first death...when she became a vampire. We grew even closer as she learned to love and trust again. She's everything to me."

Tears welled in his eyes, and he let them roll down his cheeks. "Please, Robert. They're going to make her think I'm the one torturing her. Imagine what it would do to you if the person you loved most in the world tortured you for all eternity."

Robert tilted his head, looking at him with sympathy. "I would have to get permission from the higher power. That would take a while."

Azrael looked at the clock on his phone and closed his eyes, letting out a defeated sigh. Damn the time construct here. "I have fifteen minutes left before her body will reject any attempt of reanimation."

"I'm sorry, Azrael. I don't have the authority to make an exception like that."

A sob bubbled from his chest and lodged in his throat. His eyes stung with tears, and his heart shattered into a billion pieces.

He had lost her.

CHAPTER FOURTEEN

AZRAEL GRIPPED HIS scythe, using it as leverage to heave himself from the chair. His body felt heavy, and it pained him to move. It was over. Fifteen minutes in the spirit realm would speed by quicker than a gluttony demon on his way to an all-you-can-eat buffet.

Robert remained seated, drumming

his fingers on the table. "I can't stand to see you in pain, brother."

Azrael looked at him, his vision blurring with tears. "It seems this will be my lot in life." It shouldn't have surprised him. This was exactly what he'd been protecting himself from over the past decades. Once again, his heart had broken, and this time, there would be no chance of mending it. He was a grief counselor; his *life* was grief.

Robert stood and placed his hand on Azrael's shoulder. "No. I can't let another angel suffer."

"Yet you can't let me into the spirit realm without permission from the higher power."

His new friend arched a brow. "I can't *let* you in, but with that scythe in your hand, I couldn't stop you from forcing your way inside."

Azrael's pulse sprinted, and he checked the time on his phone. Ten minutes remained. "How do I find the DMS once I'm inside?"

"It's all about intention. Imagine where you need to be, flap your wings, and you'll be there."

He shook Robert's hand. "Thank you. I owe you one."

"Your phone won't work inside. Ten minutes could feel like ten hours or ten seconds, especially in the DMS."

Azrael nodded and stepped through the forbidden door.

White mist swirled on the floor, parting as he moved forward. A dozen souls wandered around, most likely searching for their paradise, but when a woman looked at him, she gasped.

"Reaper," a man whispered, and all the souls disappeared into the fog.

"Excuse me," an angel with red hair called as she flew toward him. "You can't be in here." She landed in front of Azrael, and a flush of pink tinged her cheeks. "Oh, my, Azrael. You are exactly how..." She cleared her throat and spoke into her watch, "Robert, we've had a breach. Please escort Azrael back to his realm."

"Robert is indisposed." He gripped Severus in both hands to help with the implication.

Her lips parted on a gasp. "What did you do to him?"

He didn't have time for conversation, so he closed his eyes, imagined himself finding his destination, and flapped his wings. When he lifted his lids, he stood in the waiting room of the DMS. No one sat behind the counter, so he rang the bell.

As his impatience intensified, twenty clocks appeared on the walls, their incessant ticking taunting him. He rang the bell again, jabbing the plunger over and over until the damn thing crumbled beneath his fist.

A door stood to the left, and he grabbed the handle, jerking it up and down and ramming his shoulder against the metal. It wouldn't budge. The clocks still ticked. Were they marking the seconds? The minutes? The hours? It was impossible to tell.

What the fuck was he doing? Azrael was *the* Archangel of Death, for Lucifer's sake. He wasn't powerless here. The clock on his phone might have ceased to mark time, but intention was everything in the spirit realm.

In his current state, he could only imagine his haste was speeding up time. That simply would not do. He inhaled deeply and closed his eyes, focusing his energy in his core. As it built, he sent out a pulse of magic, filling the room with vibrating power.

The clocks stopped.

Sadly, with time standing still, he felt as if he moved through molasses. He gripped the countertop and swung himself over, the act excruciatingly slow. As his feet finally hit the floor, he breathed deeply again, centering himself. He could not let his impatience to find Deirdre get the better of him.

***

Deirdre's eyes rolled upward as the demon in the video droned on and on. His monotone voice was so torturous, she wondered if the DMS was actually her place in Hell. She'd go batshit if she had to listen to another minute of this guy's description of the various levels and torture methods.

Even Granny couldn't keep her eyes open anymore. Her head dropped forward, her chin resting against her chest, and her arm fell to her side. The ball of yarn she'd been knitting with hit the floor and rolled to Deirdre's feet.

"What am I doing? I'm a kickass vampire; I don't give up." Just because she was dead, it didn't mean she had to accept this jank-ass fate someone cooked up for her. There had to be a way out of here, and she intended to find it.

AZRAEL

Step one would be to make sure Granny couldn't alert anyone to her escape until she was long gone. She rose to her feet and picked up the yarn before tiptoeing toward her warden. The air felt heavy, a shift in the energy reminding her vaguely of the pulses Azrael would send out to communicate with spirits. Could he be there, trying to rescue her? *Yeah, right.* If dark angels could get into the spirit realm, he surely would have been there already.

It didn't matter. She was going to rescue herself.

Granny's left hand lay on the arm of the chair, so Deirdre stepped around the back and enacted her plan. Using the yarn as rope, she wound it round and round, binding Granny's arm to the chair. The woman looked as old as dirt and as fragile as a glass stiletto. It shouldn't take much to restrain her, but Deirdre wasn't taking chances.

She tied off the yarn, breaking it with her teeth before moving to her other arm. Carefully, gently, she lifted it from Granny's side and returned it to the chair. Granny snorted, lifting her head, and Deirdre yanked her hand away, ducking behind the chair and holding her breath. *Don't wake up now, you old bat.*

She settled again, her chin resting against her chest, and Deirdre continued the binding. With both arms secured to the chair, Deirdre lay on the floor and scooted beneath the desk. Granny's sandals revealed thick yellow toenails and nasty calluses on her feet. *Gross. And what's up with all these dust bunnies? Is there no custodial service in the afterlife?*

Trying not to vomit—not that she actually could since she was a ghost, but the feeling still lurched in her stomach— she bound Granny's ankles together. As she wiggled her way out from under the desk, one of the culpable bunnies tickled her nose, making her sneeze.

She slapped a hand over her mouth and froze.

Granny snorted again, jerking her head up.

Oh, man. That's it; I'm toast.

The door swung open, and Deirdre hit her head on the underside of the desk as she scrambled to her feet. It was over. The demon had come to drag her to Hell. Wait... She squeezed her eyes shut and opened them wide.

"Azrael?" Cool relief flooded her ghostly form, and she ran toward him and jumped, wrapping her legs around his waist and hugging him for all she was worth. "I thought it was impossible for dark angels to come here."

"Nothing can keep me away from you. I love you, Deirdre Boudreaux."

She planted a giant kiss on his mouth. "I love you too."

"What in heaven's name?" Granny jerked on her restraints. She spun around in her chair, and as her gaze landed on them, her eyes turned solid black. "Azrael." Her sweet grandma voice sounded more like a growl.

"Abaddon." Azrael tightened his hold on Deirdre and backed toward the door.

"You can't take her. She belongs to us now." Granny—er—Abaddon's voice pitched up and down like a demon was trying to come out of her frail old body.

Holy hellhounds. Granny was a demon?

"Over my dead body." Azrael moved his scythe, angling it across Deirdre's back.

"That can be arranged."

"Nope." Deirdre tried to move her feet to the floor, but Azrael tightened his hold even more. "One dead body is enough. Time to go." She patted his shoulder.

Granny Abaddon roared, snapping the yarn as if it were made from spider webs, and stood. Her body morphed, growing from a petite, hunched old lady into an eight-foot-tall monster with scaly black skin and obsidian eyes.

Now, if Deirdre had control of the situation, they'd have been out the door the second Granny busted through her restraints. But Azrael closed his eyes—literally closed his eyes in the face of the biggest, meanest demon she had ever seen—and took a deep breath.

"What are you doing, *cher*? We need to scoot." She patted his cheek, hoping to wake him up to the severity of their position.

Abaddon lunged, and Azrael sent out a pulse of magic, knocking the scary-as-all-get-out demon on his ass. Then he sent out another pulse, spun for the door, and ran.

Deirdre clung to him and peered over his shoulder as the demon rose and gave chase. *Jesus Christ on a bicycle!* She'd been sitting in a room with a rabid demon for the past Lilith-knew-how-long.

AZRAEL

Azrael punched a silver square on the wall, disengaging the lock, and plowed through the door.

"She's ours now, reaper!" Abaddon growled, his hooves—yep, hooves—pounding the ground as he ran after them.

The moment they busted out the DMS front door, Azrael flapped his wings and took to the sky. "Hold on tight. He's coming."

Deirdre dared a glance over his shoulder, and, sure enough, Abaddon had sprouted a set of leathery black wings. He soared toward them, and Azrael angled up, heading vertically toward what might be sky or might be ceiling; Deirdre still wasn't sure.

Abaddon followed, and he was gaining on them. *Oh, fuck.* He reached a taloned hand for Azrael's foot and yanked, sending the dark angel spiraling through the air. Deirdre slipped, and Azrael dropped his scythe to catch her with both arms. Severus disappeared into the misty floor below, and Azrael caught the air with his wings, stopping their fall.

"Don't make this harder than it has to be." Abaddon stopped two yards in front of them, both the angel and the demon hovering in place in the sky.

"I'm taking her home."

"The hell you are." With a flap, Abaddon raced toward them, and Azrael dove toward the ground.

"Severus!" Deirdre called. "I see it there."

"I'm not letting you go, so I need you to grab it." He soared two feet above the ground, and as they approached the celestial silver glinting the mist, Deirdre reached out her arms and grabbed the handle.

"Got it!"

Azrael angled up. Abaddon raced toward them. Deirdre swung Severus like a baseball bat hitting a home run, and Abaddon's lifeless body tumbled to the ground.

"What have you done?" The demon's spirit roared a split second before he was sucked into the DMS building.

Deirdre didn't have a moment to feel relief or even to comprehend everything that had happened. Azrael flew them straight for another door and out into a void. Robert the angel sat alone at a table, sipping tea, and he waved as they flew overhead.

"You might need a temporary warden in the DMS," Azrael called. "I'll be back later."

Without another word, he tucked his wings behind his back, and they fell. Sparkling crystals blurred into blinding light as the tunnel grew wider as they descended. Azrael's feet barely touched the floor when they reached bottom, then he flapped his wings again and soared over Purgatory.

"Did we make it?" she asked. "Is there still time?"

"I don't know, but we're trying regardless." They reached his front door, and he threw it open, still clutching Deirdre to his chest. Tabitha screeched as his boots pounded down the hall, and he yanked the sheet from Deirdre's naked body on the bed.

"Do it now."

She nodded and gripped his blade, lying back into her corpse. Bracing herself for the electric shock, she closed her eyes and let go.

CHAPTER FIFTEEN

"DEIRDRE?" AZRAEL HELD his breath, listening for the tell-tale snap that should have sounded when her soul rejoined with her body. She lay motionless, silent. Her body hadn't outright rejected her like it had done before, but she didn't seem very undead, either.

Tabitha jumped on the bed and meowed. Azrael shushed her, straining to hear something...anything in the silence. His heart sank into his stomach. "Deirdre, if it's not working, you can come out. We might be too late."

He leaned down and pressed a kiss to her forehead. As his lips met her skin, he heard it. A snap sounded from her chest, and she gasped. Her lids flew open, and she sucked in another breath.

"Holy mother of Cerberus!" She sat up, clutching her arms and squeezing her breasts, checking to see if she was alive. Her gaze locked on him as he set Severus aside and sank onto the bed, then she scrambled into his lap.

"I can feel your warmth again." She cupped his face in her hands, gazing into his eyes as tears welled in her own.

"I can feel you."

His throat thickened, his entire body shuddering with the overwhelming emotions. Deirdre was whole again. "I told you I would fix you once you fixed yourself."

"Hell yeah, you did." She gripped the hem of his shirt and lifted it. "Take this off. I need to feel you. I need to know this is real."

"It's real, my love." He pulled off his shirt and cradled her against his chest. Her skin had returned to cool rather than deathly cold, and as she trailed kisses along his neck and nipped his lobe, he shivered. "How do you feel?"

"Famished," she whispered into his ear. "And so fucking horny."

He chuckled. "I can take care of both."

She ran her nose from his shoulder to his neck, inhaling deeply. Then she bit.

A deep moan rolled up from his chest as her fangs pierced his flesh, and his cock hardened with lust while his heart swelled with love. He held his soulmate in his arms, and he planned to keep her forever.

After she fed, she shuddered and pulled away, her tongue slipping out to catch an errant drop of blood from the corner of her mouth. With a wicked grin, she pushed him onto his back and yanked down his zipper. He lifted his hips, helping her work his jeans down his thighs before she went for his underwear. As she yanked them off, his dick sprang to attention, and Deirdre gave it three firm strokes before circling her tongue around his tip.

Fire shot through his veins at her touch. She ran her hands up his thighs, using her body to stroke his cock as she moved in for a kiss. Her lips were soft, and a hint of copper lingered on her tongue.

"I need to be with you, Azrael," she whispered. "Make love to me."

Her cool breath on his skin raised goosebumps, and he moved to the center of the mattress, laying her on her back. Not more than twenty minutes ago, he thought he'd lost her forever. Now she was here, alive as a vampire could be. So many emotions swirled in his chest, filling him to the brim and bubbling over. He loved Deirdre. He loved her so completely, his entire body ached with need.

He gazed into her eyes as he filled

her, and she looked back at him with an expression of utter adoration. As he began to move his hips, she let out a breathy moan, running her fingers over his feathers the way she knew he loved to be touched. The sensation set his soul ablaze.

Pressing his forehead to hers, he pulled out slowly, until only his tip remained, before circling his hips and gently sliding back inside. An erotic *mmm* vibrated across her lips, and she cupped the back of his head, pulling him in for another kiss.

He made love to her slowly, savoring the delicious friction of her body squeezing him, the sensual sounds she made, the feel of her fingers running through his hair, caressing his skin and feathers. He paid attention to her reactions, her gasps for breath and her nails digging into his shoulders letting him know exactly what she needed...and he adored giving it to her.

As her breathing grew shallow, she panted into his ear, "Faster."

He pumped his hips, rising onto his arms to watch her come. She tossed her head back and gripped his forearms, and as she screamed his name, he joined her in paradise. *Their* paradise. Lowering his body to hers, he rode the wave of his orgasm, slowing his movements to bring her down gently. As he stilled, she wrapped her arms and legs around him, holding him as if she'd never let go.

***

Reluctantly, Deirdre released her grip on her dark angel and allowed him to roll to his side. She faced him, holding both his hands in hers and tangling her legs with his.

"Welcome back." Azrael smiled, and his eyes glistened.

"I'm happy to be here." She bit her bottom lip and held his gaze. This was all too good to be true, and while she was tempted to pinch herself to be certain she wasn't dreaming, she didn't dare let him go. Azrael was worth hanging on to. No more flavors of the month for her. From now on, dark, brooding, and angelic would be the only one for her.

"How did you find me? I thought dark angels were forbidden from going into the spirit realm."

He chuckled. "I had a little help from a new friend."

"Robert?"

"Indeed. Lucifer won't be thrilled to know I forced my way in, and I'm sure the light angels' higher power will be furious, but I can handle whatever consequence they want to dish out. You're worth it."

"What about Abaddon?"

He rolled his eyes as if the demon disgusted him. "I'll reanimate him."

"Won't he come after us? He seemed intent on sending me to Hell."

"Once I explain to Lucifer what happened, he won't allow retaliation. The King of Hell understands the lengths a man will go to for his soulmate."

Her stomach fluttered at his words. "Speaking of soulmates..."

"You are mine, Deirdre. I hope you can believe that after everything you've gone through."

She nodded. "I do. I know we belong together."

He leaned in and took her mouth with his. His warmth, his cinnamon scent, the feel of his hands skimming her hip as they kissed... There was no doubt Purgatory...no, Azrael...was her paradise.

"Will you stay with me forever?" He cupped her face in his hand and ran his thumb over her swollen lips. "Will you be my wife?"

"Of course I will. Forever and ever." She laughed. "I'd say 'til death do us part, but seeing as how I've already died twice..."

"Yeah, that's not happening."

"Never again. I'm yours."

Thank you for reading!

Watch your favorite online retailer for the other books in the Speed Dating with the Denizens of the Underworld series.

Turn the page now for an excerpt from *Samael by Julie Morgan*, Book Four in the Speed Dating with the Denizens of the Underworld series!

Follow our Facebook page here: <u>Speed Dating with the Denizens of the Underworld Series</u>

EXCERPT

When innocence meets darkness...

ISABELLA STOOD IN the center of his den, a cardinal of hope amongst the demons of Hell... literally.

She was breathtaking in her strapless red dress. The shape of the upper bodice made his mouth salivate with the desire to take her, here and now. Samael would need to take things a little slower than what he was typically used to.

At Den of Sin, the women and men would fall to their knees for him, begging to please him in any way possible. Some wanted to feel accepted in a world where they were denied this from their family and friends. The lines of acceptance and envy crossed in varying degrees, but Samael enjoyed exploiting the line in the sand, so to speak.

Hand a silver platter of what was most desired, from being told "you're perfect" to a simple "well done" could send a tittering person over the brink into disaster mode. And that's the playground Samael enjoyed frequenting most, corrupting those who were easily corruptible.

Then there were the ones who were the thrill of the hunt, the ones who were harder to possess. He longed for those every once in a while, and it had been a while since he pursued anything worthwhile.

As he eyed Isabella standing motionless in his home, a soft grin played across his lips. She was so soft, innocent, exuding desire in waves that he could find himself drowning in. He just needed to figure out a way to break through her barrier and sink this unsinkable ship.

Watch for the other books in the
Speed Dating with the Denizens of the
Underworld Series

AZRAEL

Loki

Lilith

The Morrígan

Orion

Hera

Abel

Odin

Mormos

Zeus

Michael

Váli

Apollo

Raphael

Baldur

Poseidon

Gabrielle

Frigg

Uriel

And More!

CARRIE PULKINEN

For more supernatural fun, check out Carrie's other books in the Speed Dating With the Denizens of the Underworld Series.
https://carriepulkinen.com/speed-dating-with-the-denizens-of-the-underworld/

***

Signup for my newsletter and get a free copy of Sweet Release...
carriepulkinen.com/subscribe/

***

More from Carrie Pulkinen

carriepulkinen.com

Facebook

Instagram

TikTok

AZRAEL

If you enjoyed this book, you may also
enjoy...

New Orleans Nocturnes

Crescent City Wolf Pack

Crescent City Ghost Tours

Haunted Ever After

The Rest of Forever

Sign Steal Deliver

Flipping the Bird

Soul Catchers

ABOUT CARRIE PULKINEN

Carrie Pulkinen is a paranormal romance author who has always been fascinated with things that go bump in the night. Of course, when you grow up next door to a cemetery, the dead (and the undead) are hard to ignore. Pair that with her passion for writing and her love of a good happily-ever-after, and becoming a paranormal romance author seems like the only logical career choice. Before she decided to turn her love of the written word into a career, Carrie spent the first part of her professional life as a high school journalism and yearbook teacher. She loves good chocolate and bad puns, and in her free time, she likes to read, drink wine, and travel with her family.